BRIGHAM'S WAY

Brigham, Seth and Jacob Tyler came to the Colorado badlands in search of gold. They found it alright — but they also found it took a deal of holding onto. There were violent killers ready to take it from them . . . and the three brothers would have to match bullet for bullet for each of them to retain his wealth, and forge his own way in life.

RICHARD WYLER

BRIGHAM'S WAY

Complete and Unabridged

LINFORD
Leicester

First published in Great Britain in 1976

First Linford Edition
published 2007

The moral right of the author has been asserted

British Library CIP Data

Wyler, Richard
    Brigham's Way.—Large print ed.—
Linford western library
1. Western stories
2. Large type books
I. Title II. Jordan, Matt, *1940* –
823.9'14 [F]

ISBN 978–1–84617–778–1

Published by
F. A. Thorpe (Publishing)
Anstey, Leicestershire

Set by Words & Graphics Ltd.
Anstey, Leicestershire
Printed and bound in Great Britain by
T. J. International Ltd., Padstow, Cornwall

This book is printed on acid-free paper

1

Late on a hot, dry day in mid-summer we came up the rough trail and drew rein on the crest of a slope, looking down on the booming gold-camp of Hope, Colorado. We had ridden some considerable distance that day and were glad to have finally reached our destination.

There were five of us, including myself. My name is Brigham Tyler, late by thirteen years of the county of Lancashire in England, and with me were my brothers Seth and Jacob. The other two who made up our number were an oldtimer named Sachs, one of the hardluck prospectors who'd been doing the rounds for more years than even he could remember, and Joel Welcome, a young man fresh from the East, come to try his luck in the goldfields.

We were a dusty, dirty group on equally dusty horses. We were tired and hungry, having been on the trail for over a week, and all we wanted at the moment were baths and some food. Chance was that we might get neither, for goldcamps were not exactly overly concerned with these priorities. Not that we expected the height of luxury. All we needed was water to wash with and food to eat. Somewhere in the mushrooming town of buildings and tents we might find what we wanted.

Setting our mounts down the dust-thick trail we shortly brought ourselves into Hope and rode along the crowded main street. There were men everywhere, of every shape and size, and of a mixture of nationalities. We heard snatches of conversations in half a dozen languages before we were half-way down the street. There was an air of excitement about the place that was felt the moment we entered, and I could hardly hold back my own enthusiasm.

As we rode by a large, gaudy wooden building Sachs drew rein. He slid from his saddle and led his horse over to the hitch-rail, making room for his animal.

'I figure this is where I'll take my leave of you boys,' he said. 'I got me a terrible thirst that needs seein' to!'

Seth glanced up at the saloon's big sign. He ran a big hand across his own dry lips and it seemed he might join Sachs. Then he saw me watching him and his unshaven face split into a wide grin. 'No. You're right, Brig. A bath and a meal first.'

'I guess we'll see you around, Mister Sachs,' I said.

'Why you surely will, boy,' the old man said. 'Now you fellers take it easy. We come a way together an' I like you, so don't get in any trouble. Camps like this have some pretty mean characters wandering around.'

'We'll watch out,' I told him, and raised a hand as Sachs turned and went into the saloon.

Jacob had stopped a passing miner

and was asking the way to go about getting a bath and a shave. We were in luck it appeared. A barbershop had opened a week ago and it had a bath-house out back. If a man had the money to pay he could get himself as clean as he wanted. It sounded alright so we made our way down the crowded street until we reached the barbershop.

We dismounted and tied our horses, took our rifles and went into the place. It had been built of raw lumber and you could smell the unseasoned wood. It was not unpleasant. Inside it smelled of soap and hair oil and boiling water. There was one man being shaved and another waiting. The barber glanced up as we entered, and I wondered what he thought as he saw us, for we must have looked a sight with our shaggy hair and unshaven faces.

'Take a seat, boys,' he said, 'and I'll be with you directly.'

'Anybody using the bath-house?' Jacob asked.

'No. You boys want to give her a try?'

'You said it.'

The barber gave a shout and a small, moon-faced Chinese came out of the back. 'Four customers, Lee. By the looks of 'em you better get a heap of water to boiling!'

The Chinese grinned. He was all teeth. 'All come,' he sing-songed, and we followed him through to the rear of the barbershop.

The bath-house was just an extension containing a large, wood-fired boiler and four large wooden tubs big enough to take two men each. The Chinese yelled something in his own tongue and two more of his countrymen appeared. The three of them began to hurry around with buckets of boiling water.

We stood and watched them for a while. Then Seth put down his rifle and started in to take his boots off.

'Hell,' he said, 'we didn't come to watch.'

That did it, and before long the four of us were out of our clothes and hopping around in water hot enough to curl

5

your toes. The Chinese handed us blocks of rough yellow soap. It took a lot of scrubbing to get a lather, but it was worth it, for by the time we emerged our naked bodies were as pink as boiled lobsters. While we'd washed the Chinese had taken our clothes outside and had done a fair job of cleaning off the dust that had collected.

Dressed again we went back into the barbershop and took turns to be shaved and trimmed. When we finally stepped out onto the street again we looked and felt like different men.

'I can face a meal now,' I said.

'There's a place across the street,' Jacob said.

We crossed over and went inside. It was no more than a large tent that housed long tables and benches, with food prepared down at the far end. The place wasn't too busy and we had plenty of room.

A thin-faced man with deep-set eyes and pale hair shuffled listlessly over to us. 'What you got?' I asked.

'Beans an' venison.'

Now I'm not averse to beans or venison, but we'd eaten little else for the past week, and the thought of more of the same was by no means welcome. I heard Jacob groan.

'You got anything else?'

He shook his head. 'No. You want it?'

I glanced round the table. Nobody said a word. 'We'll have it. For four,' I said. 'And plenty of coffee.'

'I think Sachs had the best idea,' Seth remarked. 'Hell, I'd have thought they'd have some beef.'

'Don't even mention beef,' Jacob grumbled. He slumped forward on the table and stared out at the busy street. 'I wonder if they got any women in this town?'

I grinned. Jacob was a real ladies man. Not that you'd think so when you saw him, for he was not what you'd call handsome. But he was big, like both Seth and me, and he had a natural way about him that was liable to have the ladies flocking round like ants at a

7

honeypot. Seth was steadier with women, and me, being the youngest, though interested, I was still awkward in their presence.

Joel, who had been staring out at the street since we'd sat down, said: 'There's one, Jacob,' and he pointed.

We all glanced up. Joel was right. Across the street a dark-haired girl in a yellow dress was strolling casually along, and even from this distance it was plain that she was a pretty good-looking female.

'Keep my beans warm,' Jacob said, pushing to his feet. He glanced round at Seth and me, grinning at us. 'I'll be back.' He stepped away from the table and left the tent, crossing the busy street with long strides. He reached the girl and we saw him sweep his hat off in a grand gesture. For a moment he stood talking to the girl, and then they moved off up the street, out of our sight, with the girl hanging onto Jacob's arm like she'd known him for years.

'That Jacob!' Seth grinned. 'I tell

you, Brig, women will bring him nothing but trouble.'

I smiled. 'He's already found that out, but it doesn't stop him. Anyway, Seth, he's full grown. He knows his own mind so don't worry over him.'

Our food came then and we put aside conversation to concentrate on eating. The beans were tasteless and the venison not as fresh as it could be. If we hadn't been as hungry as we were I don't think we would have touched the stuff. Even the coffee was bitter, but at least it was hot and strong. We emerged from the place with full stomachs but little satisfaction.

'What do we do now, Seth?' I asked. By this time we had climbed back onto our horses.

'I figure we should find someplace to make camp for tonight. Somewhere out of town. Come morning we'll start and look for a place to stake our claim.'

'What about Jacob?' Joel asked.

'I'll find him,' Seth said. 'You two go and have a look round town. I'll take

Jacob's horse and let him know what we're going to do. He can join us later.'

He took the reins of Jacob's horse and led off back up the street, leaving me and Joel to our own devices.

'You feel like a drink?' I asked.

Joel nodded. His eyes were bright with excitement as he stared around. I knew how he felt, for I was eager for a look myself. We rode along the street until we spotted a likely saloon. We hitched our horses, took our rifles with us, and went inside.

The place was crowded and we had to shove our way to the bar, which was nothing more than planks on the top of empty beer kegs. Finding a space we squeezed in and I ordered a couple of beers. I'd never taken to hard liquor and Joel would drink nothing but beer. When it came we drank deeply, for we both had a strong thirst.

I gazed around me. Whoever owned this place must have been making himself a tidy pile of money and it came to me then that digging up the gold was only one way to get rich. Supplying the needs of the miners, whether it was drink or food or tools, was an aspect of Hope that needed studying. I'd come here with the intention of looking for gold, but that didn't rule out taking other things into consideration. I had made myself a promise some years back that I was going to make my way in this country. I had no intention of wasting my life, and while I was not over-educated, I did have a sound outlook on life and I'd learned a long time ago to keep my eyes open, to watch and learn and remember.

A sudden outburst of noise caught my attention. Over on the other side of the saloon a knot of men abruptly broke apart and I was able to see the cause of the upset. A card game had erupted into sudden violence and two men faced each other over the table. I couldn't make out what was being said, but it was obvious that the two were in some disagreement. One of the men pointed at the cards on the table and mouthed something to the other. This one, scarlet-faced, stepped away from the table, his hand going to his right hip. Almost before we knew it guns were firing, the sound drowning every voice in the place. The scarlet-faced man pitched to the floor, his chest bloody, and his opponent clutched a hand to an arm that was limp and bleeding. As the gunfire died away men surged around the pair. The downed man, who was obviously dead, was picked up and carried out. The wounded victor left under his own steam, escorted by at least a dozen spectators. Within a couple of minutes the incident had been forgotten and the saloon returned to its noisy state.

I had seen my first boom-camp violence. I didn't know it then but it would not be the last time I saw violence in Hope, nor did I know how deeply I would get myself involved in it. Had I known this I would not have been so unconcerned.

Joel was looking at me over his beer

glass. His face was pale and he looked sick.

'You alright?' I asked.

'First time I ever saw a man killed,' he said.

'Don't let it bother you. Man isn't human who doesn't get sick at the sight of something like that.' I finished my beer and put down my glass. 'Let's get out of here,' I suggested.

We took our leave of the saloon and got on our horses, turning them to take us out of town. As we moved off I caught sight of the signboard outside the saloon. It was called The Bucket of Blood!

A short ride got us clear of Hope and we found ourselves riding up into the hills. All around us were signs of the human invasion. Tents and small cabins were dotted here and there. There were wagons and rigs, horses and mules, and we even saw one wagon being drawn by a team of oxen. Smoke from scores of fires rose into the air. The lure of gold had brought people by the hundreds to

Hope, and maybe for some of them that's what it was. Hope! For the future. For a better life. And for some it would be. Some would find their dream, their pot of gold. But others would leave with no more than they had when they arrived, and in some cases they would leave with less.

We rode until we found a place that was fairly well untouched. A stream ran close by and there were trees. There was grass for the horses. We got down and tethered our mounts. I began to build a fire while Joel unsaddled. By the time he'd finished I had a good fire going. I went to the stream for water and put some coffee on to boil.

After that I sat down and rolled a smoke. Joel shook his head when I offered him the makings. He'd been pretty quiet since we'd left town and I asked what was troubling him.

'You must think me yellow acting the way I did over that shooting,' he said and I realised it had been preying on his mind.

I lit my smoke. Taking off my hat I ran my hand through my hair. 'Joel, you are talking like a damn fool. I don't think for one minute that you're yellow. We've known each other long enough to be able to tell what the other's like, and I know how you are. How do you think I feel? I'll tell you. I felt the same as you. The same as I always feel when I see a man shot. I felt sick. Maybe I didn't show it but I sure felt it. I felt it every time I saw a man shot during the war. A man sees enough he gets to accepting it but he still feels it inside. If he don't then he ought to be dead himself, 'cause when he can't react it means he's gone cold, lost his feelings, and that's as good as being dead. Joel, don't you let anyone tell you it's yellow to show how you feel.'

He glanced at me, his face almost angry. 'Brig, next time you tell me you have no education I'll hit you! By God, I wish I'd had your chance at life!'

'My chance? The only chances I got were the ones I took myself. Seth and

Jacob and me come to this country thirteen years ago from England. I was nine when we jumped the ship we'd joined at Liverpool. We worked from the day we landed. Took any job that came along. Soon as we could we headed West and got in with any cow outfit that would tolerate us. Didn't do too bad but then we didn't do too well either. By the time I was fifteen I knew pretty well most there was to learn about cattle. About then we decided to try setting up on our own. Hadn't been at it more'n a year when the war come along. I was nineteen when we joined the Union Army. I reckon we were lucky. We managed to stick together all the way through and we came out without anything more serious than a few odd scars here and there. When we got back home we found our spread wasn't ours any more. We were down in Texas and while we'd been away a bunch of Comancheros had moved in. We had to fight them to get it back. I suppose we could have started again but the place was different. So we drifted for a while, got in a few scrapes, then heard about the strike here and decided to try our luck.'

I reached for a mug of coffee. I needed it. Talking in such long sentences isn't my strong suit, and I figured I'd made a considerable speech.

'And that,' I finished, 'is my 'chance'. I figure most folk could better it without trying. You foremost.'

'You're wrong, Brig,' Joel said. 'Alright, maybe I've the advantage of position, wealth, schooling, but I don't think all of that put together can better what you've had. Experience, Brig. Experience. That's what you've had and what I lack. All my life I've lived in my father's shadow. He's that kind of man. He dominates and smothers everything he owns and controls. Brig, in all my life I've never had to face a challenge, never had to come face to face with a situation that depended on my own judgement for its outcome.' He stared down into the fire, his face bitter. 'You

17

talk about being in the war. I wanted to fight for my country but I wasn't allowed. My father pulled strings so I was exempted from duty. I tried to join on my own but my father hired men to bring me back. I was watched until the war ended. Then my father decided it was time to call his watchdogs off. He had plans for me to join him. To get me ready to step into his shoes. He even told me he'd picked out the girl for me to marry. That did it. I'd had enough. I didn't say anything. One night I packed my bag and left. I came West, and I made myself a promise that I wouldn't go back until I'd made my way. Until I could meet my father on equal terms. Until I can tell him I don't walk in any man's shadow.'

I poured him a mug of coffee and handed it to him.

'You'll make it, Joel, so don't fret.'

He took the coffee, his face relaxing now as he said: 'You think so, Brig?'

'Hell, yes. Couple of years from now you and me, why we'll be able to buy and sell a place like Hope just for something to do.'

He grinned then, a laugh following, and I joined him. We were still laughing when Jacob and Seth rode into camp. They looked unusually grim and when I asked why my own good humour left me fast.

'Jacob had to kill a man!' Seth said. 'He busted in on a fellow who was giving Sachs a hard time. The upshot was that Jacob got pulled down on but he was still faster. The other fellow got a shot off that missed but Jacob didn't. Got him fair and square.'

'You alright?' I asked Jacob.

He nodded. 'Hell of a mess I made of our first day.'

I handed him some coffee. 'It was you or him.'

'I guess.'

I had a feeling they hadn't told me everything. I voiced my feelings and Seth told me the rest.

'It was Cole Prentise that Jacob killed.'

'I know that name from somewhere,' I said.

'Prentise ran with a real wild bunch. Couple of hardcases run it. Red Karver and Will Pike. And they got Tall Lyons with them.'

I saw trouble brewing on the horizon. If what Seth had said was true, then we were in trouble deep. And it was trouble of the kind that was only cured with a quick mind and a quicker gun.

2

During the war Red Karver and Will Pike had run with one of the so-called Freedom Fighters Bands, who were supposed to be riding for the South but in fact they were nothing more than renegades who raided and looted, taking whatever they wanted and causing a deal more misery than the real war. After the war Karver and Pike just carried on with what they were doing. They gathered a bunch of real roughs and moved West, bringing their brand of dirty dealing with them to the gold-camps where the pickings were plentiful. In the lawless boom towns, where a man was his own law, Karver and Pike were feared names. They were said to have killed a number of men in various camps. It was probably true but nothing was ever done about it. A man kept his suspicions to himself, kept on digging, and if he made a good strike he hoped he could make his pile and get out before Karver and Pike found out and moved in. Some were lucky. Others were not. Some took savage beatings then sold out. There were the ones who stood up to the Karver-Pike bullies. They were the ones who suddenly vanished, or were found dead in some gully, most of them with bullets in the backs.

These then were the men with whom we were liable to be involved with. If Karver and Pike were operating around Hope, then we were in for an uneasy time. Not that it overly bothered Seth or Jacob or me for we had known trouble for most of our lives and took it as it came.

'Last I heard Karver and Pike were up around the Comstock,' I said to Seth. We were sitting round the fire, drinking coffee and trying to figure what might come of Jacob's killing of Cole Prentise.

'I talked to a miner,' Seth told me,

'and he said that Karver's bunch has been hanging out around Hope for nigh on six months. Seems that a vigilante group started up on the Comstock and got some hangropes filled. Seems that Karver and Pike felt the shadow of the noose a little and decided to move on.'

'Well if they come too close they'll feel more than a coil of rope,' Jacob said abruptly. His tone showed that he was angry, and when Jacob got angry he also got deadly serious, meaning every word he said.

'Go easy, brother,' I told him, 'they ain't here yet!'

He threw a scowling glance at me. Then he saw the smile on my face and he mellowed.

'You know, Joel, to hear Brig talking you'd get to believing he was the most peace-loving of us all. But he isn't. Why he's fighting mad under that smile.'

'Not at all,' I said. 'I don't go looking for trouble, but I'll not walk away when it comes.'

Joel, who had been silently sitting by,

glanced at me. 'I hope I have it in me to do the same if I ever have to face trouble myself,' he said.

Jacob put up a hand. 'Rider coming.'

I could hear the approaching horse myself now and I eased off. 'It's only Sachs,' I told them, for I'd recognised the step of Sachs' tired old dun. The animal had a slight limp and it made a distinct hoofbeat.

Moments later the old man rode into camp and dismounted. He tied his horse and then joined us at the fire. He had a bulging flour-sack in his arms and he dumped it on the ground.

'Any coffee left?' he asked.

It was getting dark now, and it wasn't until Sachs joined us at the fire that I saw his face. It was plain that Jacob had stepped in at the right time. Sach's face was bruised and cut from jaw to hairline, his skin puffed and raw. His lips were swollen and split, and his left eye was almost shut.

'Seems that Jacob did everybody a favour shooting Prentise,' I said.

Sachs nodded. 'Damn right he did! Wouldn't be sittin' here now if he hadn't come into that saloon. Man, that bastard Prentise was a mean son. He like to stomped me, an' all because I spilt his beer.'

'You mean he did that to you just for a glass of beer?' Joel's voice was shocked and I realised that he'd had more than his fair share of violence for one day.

'There's only one thing to remember, Joel,' I said. 'This isn't New York. There are no policemen out here. The Law is spread very thin and in a place like Hope the only kind is what a man carries on his hip or in his fists. It may be hard to take but it's something you should learn fast. Get in trouble and most times you only have yourself to depend on. You have a gun, then learn to use it, and be ready to use it, because others will. Don't worry over the other fellow because he sure won't be worried over you. Long as you're in the right, don't hesitate. If a man's going to kill you the only thing you got to figure is whether you can shoot first.'

'He's right, boy,' Sachs said. 'Most probably makes us sound nothing but a bunch of savages, but it's the only set of rules we got out here yet. Law'll come one day but 'til it does every man is his own law, like Brig says. It's a rough country and a man has to be rough to stay alive in it.'

Joel listened and nodded. 'I came here to make my way,' he said, 'but I guess I didn't realise just how rough it was going to be. I'll just have to learn, because I'm not going back!'

We sat for a while longer. I steered the talk away from what had taken place today and the others took up the cue. Seth broached the subject of where we should start digging and before long we were all giving our views. Here both Sachs and Joel came into their own. Sachs knew about prospecting from personal experience, while Joel was able to hold forth from his knowledge of geology, a subject he had studied for years. Between them they cornered the major part of the discussion and it took us through three more pots of coffee. It must have been close to midnight when we turned in.

I moved my blankets some distance from the fire and made sure I'd got my rifle and handgun close by.

I lay for some considerable time before I slept. My mind was full of the things that happened and my thoughts of what tomorrow would bring. Would we make a go of this hunting for gold? What would come our way from Red Karver and his crew? I stirred restlessly, wishing to get answers to my questions so I could sleep. Eventually I did sleep, but then only lightly and I woke often, to any sound that broke through to me. I finally drifted off a couple of hours before dawn. When I opened my eyes again the sky was already streaked with daylight, and Sachs was up, tending the fire. He glanced round at me as I sat up, and his face creased into a smile.

'Boy, you had a restless night.' He

brought me some coffee. 'I could hear you tossing and turning from where I was.'

'I keep you awake?'

'No. I don't sleep a lot. My age a man gets so he don't need as much as he used to.'

I got up and drank my coffee, then wandered over to the stream. I took off my shirt and had a wash. The water was cold and it made me gasp, but I felt wide awake when I got back to camp.

Sachs had everybody else up by then. He was rooting around in the sack he'd brought with him the night before and when he emptied it we thought we were seeing things. He produced a side of bacon, flour, a bag of coffee, and four cans of peaches.

'Where in hell did you get all this?' Jacob asked.

Sachs grinned. 'One of the advantages of being in this game a long time is that you know where to go to get the things you want. Mind, I had to pay for 'em but I figure it was worth it.'

We breakfasted well on bacon, beans and pancakes that Sachs made with flour and water. After the meal we checked our gear and filled our canteens from the stream.

We had decided to ride on up into the hills, well above any of the other claims. Sachs and Joel had both agreed that we might stand a better chance of finding something up there. They made a try at explaining why, but they lost me right at the start.

The sun was hot as we set out and it got hotter as we rode. As we moved higher into the hills we were able to look back on the jumble of the campsites and the claims below. Even further back we could see Hope, a maze of dark shapes that stood out against the dun-coloured earth.

We rode for over two hours. Every so often Sachs and Joel would get down and poke about in the dirt. They would pick up chunks of rock, inspect them, and toss them aside. Then we would ride on. It went on this way for some time. And then they found something.

By this time we were riding in an area of jumbled rock and tough scrub. The hills towered above us on every side. Much higher than where we were, I could see the dark green of trees and I wondered what it would be like to ride up in that country. I had heard that there were icy streams and green meadows up in the tall hills. Places where it was so peaceful a man had to shout to let himself know that he was still alive. Up there it was green and silent and the air was bright and fresh and so clear a man could see for miles. I had heard that country like this was called the High Lonesome, and though I had never yet ridden in it myself, I knew that name was the only one to describe such places. I made a promise to myself to take a ride up there some time in the near future.

But right there and then I was forced to cut short my dreaming as I heard Sachs give a shout. I drew my eyes from the distant hills and swung down out of my saddle. Jacob and Seth were already bending over Sachs and Joel.

'What is it?' I asked.

'Why, Brig, don't you know gold when you see it?' Joel said. He was holding a hunk of rock in his hand and he thrust it at me.

It looked like a chunk of crumbling rock to me at first, but then I saw the zig-zag threads of golden colour running through it. I felt my heart pound. I turned it over and over in my hand.

'You sure?' I asked.

'It's real,' Joel assured me.

'You mean we've struck gold? Just like that? Ride out and look round for a while, then just pick it up off the ground?' I must have sounded awful cynical but I couldn't help it.

Joel grinned. His young face was shiny with sweat and grimed with dirt. 'It has happened,' he said. 'What we've found, Brig, is a chunk of rock that's been washed down the hill from up above. I'll admit it's a lucky find but it doesn't mean we can quit looking. What we have to do now is to trace this back to its source.' He pointed up the rocky hillside. 'Up yonder somewhere is the place this came from. All we have to do is to find it. We might find it tomorrow, we may have to look for a week. And then we might find there isn't any gold worth bothering about.'

I tipped my hat back. 'Well that's me told!' I shaded my eyes and looked to the hillside above us. 'You figure we might find something?'

'From what I can tell this looks like pretty good stuff,' Sachs said. 'We might have hit a strong seam. Then again it might only be a foot deep.'

Jacob stood up. 'Only one way to find out,' he said. 'We go to it.'

And go to it we did. For the next week. A week in which we worked harder than we'd worked before. Under Joel's knowing eye we traced that chunk of rock back up that hill until I thought we were going to end up on the high peaks themselves. We dug and we sifted and we dug some more. At night we fell into our blankets and slept the sleep of the dead. By the end of the week we had begun to show some results. A small leather pouch was pretty well filled with gold-bearing rock. Joel explained that we were following a runoff that wound its way down from the hills and that somewhere on its journey it was passing over a gold seam and sometimes it was bringing down chunks of the gold-bearing rock. All we had to do was to find the place where the gold originated. It sounded easy but it was far from that.

We were two days into the second week when we found what we were seeking. Joel brought us together and showed us the outcropping of rock that held more of the thin gold threads. He chipped some off and passed it round.

'And now we dig!' he grinned.

We dug. Dug until our bodies ached and our fingers and palms were raw and blistered, our eyes and throats sore from the dust. We took that hillside and we opened it up and ripped out its guts.

We cut timbers to stop it falling in on us and we dug right inside that hill, so deep that we had to light lamps it was so dark. We dug for days, for nights, and the weeks slid by and before we knew it we'd been digging for a whole month.

But we had our gold. It didn't seem a lot for the amount of work but we had it. Pure, hard gold. We had a dozen canvas bags of it. Joel figured it might bring us in about forty thousand dollars. When he told me I didn't even smile. I was so tired and sick of digging that I would have given it all up just to be able to rest and maybe never see another shovel in my life. It wasn't that I'm scared of hard work. I thrive on it. But I wasn't used to grubbing around in the dark, deep earth. It was a job like this that had killed my father back in Lancashire. It was one of the reasons why Seth and Jacob and me had left. We'd come to this country to work but what we were doing now didn't sit right with me.

Joel saw my discontent and asked me about it.

'The idea sounded good,' I told him, 'but this isn't our kind of life, Joel. Seth and Jacob are like me. We like the outdoors. It's been our way since we came to this country and I guess it's in our blood.'

'You pulling out?' Joel asked.

I nodded. 'All I want is enough to get me started.'

I told Seth and Jacob what I'd decided. They both said I was to do what I wished. Both of them had figured on giving the mining a few more weeks. We decided that I should take my share of the gold and that I would retain a share in the mine's future output. I wasn't very keen on the last part but they said that was how it would be.

The next day Seth and I were left alone at the mine while Jacob and Sachs and Joel rode down to Hope. They were going for supplies and then Jacob and Joel would carry on from

Hope and ride to the capitol to file our claim.

I'd said that I would stay until they got back in a week or so even though I was eager to make a start on my own plans.

Seth had gone off to cut some wood. I settled down at the mine entrance, my rifle at hand, and picked up a book that Joel had lent me.

It was a little past noon when something made me look up. I came to my feet, grabbing my rifle.

A bunch of riders were coming down off a low ridge, heading straight for camp. There were eight of them, hard-looking men and all armed to the teeth. I got a feeling their visit was less than neighbourly.

I noticed that the one in the lead, a big, heavy man, who had hair and a moustache of red, reminded me of someone. And after a few seconds I knew that I was looking at Red Karver!

I stepped out into the open and waited for them to ride up to me and I knew that it was trouble that was riding in. I jacked a round into my rifle's chamber, holding the weapon easy, but in plain sight. If they'd come hunting for trouble then trouble was what they would get. And I was in the right frame of mind to give it to them.

3

They drew rein some yards from me and for a moment we eyed each other in silence. Red Karver sat his horse a little in front of his men, though two riders were close by him. I took these to be Will Pike and Tall Lyons, and like Karver they looked to be mean, hard men.

Karver tipped his dirty hat back and eased himself into a more comfortable position in his saddle. 'What they call you, boy?' he asked.

'Brigham Tyler, if it's any of your business, Karver.'

He leaned forward. 'You know me?'

'I heard your name,' I told him. 'It supposed to do something to me?'

'He talks big,' said one of Karver's companions.

Karver grinned. 'Maybe you ought to go down there and show him he ain't as big as he thinks, Tall.'

Tall Lyons nodded. He was a big man, at least six-six and nearly as broad. He looked at me now and I saw his eyes were as pale as frozen spring water.

'I'd call him off, Karver,' I said, 'because if he puts one foot on my land I'll lay a bullet straight between his eyes. And if you think I'm fooling just let him keep coming.'

Something in my voice must have told them I wasn't fooling. Tall Lyons stayed in his saddle but his eyes bored into me in a way that almost hurt.

'Before you ride out you can tell me what you came for.'

'Heard you'd made a strike. Come to make you an offer for the claim. In cash. You could be on your way by nightfall.'

I smiled at him. 'You really got that off well,' I said. 'How many times have you made that speech before you shot a man in the back?'

Karver spat suddenly. 'Damn you,

boy, I'm giving you a chance to get out easy.'

'I prefer to stay. I got four partners and I know they don't want to sell out. More so to a load of scum like you and your crew, so I'd ride out now. Before some of you get hurt.'

'By God, he's got nerve, I'll give him that,' said the one I judged to be Will Pike. He was thin and almost girlish in his way but he looked as deadly as a poised cottonmouth.

'I've more than nerve,' I said. 'I've a loaded rifle and I know how to use it.'

'You any good?' Pike asked, sizing me up.

'As good as my brother Jacob. Cole Prentise could testify to that if he wasn't dead.'

'Yeah! I'll settle with him later,' Karver said.

'You're not out of this yet,' I told him.

'One man,' Karver grinned. 'One man?'

'Two!' The voice came from behind

me, and I recognised Seth's deep tones.

'They come to buy us out, Seth.'

'So I heard.'

'Trouble is I can't convince them we don't figure to sell.'

Seth appeared at my side, his rifle in his big hands. He faced Red Karver and looked him over. 'Can't you understand English, mister?'

Karver stiffened. It was plain to see that he wasn't used to talk like this. Everyone was supposed to jump when he spoke, not talk back. He didn't like it and I got the feeling he was a little unsure of us. The trouble was that with a situation like this before him, Karver was liable to do something rash. His influence depended on the tough, violent image he had built up. He couldn't afford to let that image become tarnished.

I saw this in the way he reacted to Seth's words and I knew that he wasn't about to let it lie. I watched him close but didn't let my attention wander far from the rest of the crew with him. It was a move that probably saved Seth and me from being cut down.

At first it seemed as if Karver had quit, for he yanked his horse's head around, as if he was about to ride off, but I saw one of his men look towards him, saw Karver's head nod slightly. I saw the man tense and drop his hand to his holstered handgun and I knew that if I didn't act fast Seth and I would be dead men within seconds.

'Down, Seth!' I yelled, and saw him drop into the dust as I went down myself. As I bellied down I had my rifle ready, thrusting it forward and tilting it up. I still had my eye on the man who'd gone for his gun. Our move had caught him off-guard but he had his gun out and it wouldn't take him long to adjust his aim. I saw sunlight flash on his gun's barrel as he drew down on Seth and I shot him. I fired once and my bullet took him in the chest and drove him from the saddle.

Moments later it was as if all hell had broken loose. Karver's crew went for their guns and the peaceful hills exploded with noise. Seth and I moved our positions the moment I'd fired, and though we only had seconds we found enough cover to protect ourselves as we exchanged shots with Karver and his crew. Dust fogged the air as nervous horses jostled each other and made a general confusion.

I emptied two more saddles and Seth put one down and placed a bullet in another man's arm.

Bullets struck the ground around Seth and me but we came through without being touched. Maybe we had taken Karver's crew too much by surprise. Whatever it was it gave us the upper hand and we took full advantage of it.

Of a sudden the firing stopped. Karver's crew put up their guns and we all faced each other in an uneasy silence. I shoved to my feet and stepped forward, my rifle still held ready. I guessed they had figured it wasn't worth any more dead men, especially with the dead ones being their own companions.

'Now that was a damn fool trick, Karver,' I said harshly. 'I figured you for a man with more sense. Seems I was wrong. You're just plain stupid. Now you pick up your dead and get the hell off this land fast!'

When the dead men had been draped across their saddles and his crew had turned their horses away, Karver eased his horse forward. His face was dark with anger, his thick-lipped mouth taut. I knew I'd made a bad enemy in Red Karver — but it didn't bother me overly. In this country a man learned to live with such things and to face them when they came hunting for trouble.

'I won't forget this, Tyler,' he said. 'This is the second time I've been crossed by your kin and there'll be a settlin' one day soon.'

'Any time,' Seth said quietly.

'Now move out,' I added and Karver turned his horse away with a heavy hand.

Will Pike was the last man to go. He glanced at me as he gathered his reins. His face bore a faintly sardonic expression.

'You said you were good,' he remarked, 'and you proved it. I just wonder if you're good enough to last.'

'I'll be there come the day,' I told him and I knew that eventually I would have to face him with a gun.

Pike straightened his hat and rode out after Karver.

Seth and I watched them as they slowly rode away and neither of us moved until they were well and truly out of sight.

'It was never like this when we were running beef,' I said and Seth looked at me and grinned.

We built a fire and brewed coffee. As we sat drinking we talked over what had happened. We agreed that it was going to be advisable to have someone on watch from now on. Karver would want to hit back at us. That fact was clear. We'd hurt him badly and he wouldn't take it lying down. I began to feel guilty about leaving but Seth said I should still go. I had my plans and a right to carry them through if I had a mind to. He said that once the others were back things would be better.

When Jacob and Joel did return, nearly ten days later, they listened to our tale in silence, Joel reacting as I'd expected him to. He still wasn't able to take in the sudden violence of this wild country. I hoped for his sake that he would be able to conquer this feeling soon, for he might one day be faced with personal violence, and there might not be anyone handy to help pull him out of it.

Jacob took the news differently. He was put out because of what he'd missed. 'I hope he tries again,' he said and I could tell by his tone that he was dearly hoping they would.

I stayed with them for a few more days, helping with some heavy digging. But I was eager to be on my way and I told Seth that I was ready to go. That evening after supper Joel handed me one of the gold-bearing sacks.

'Your share of what we've got up to now,' he said. 'Should be around eight thousand dollars, more or less.'

'Enough for what I want,' I said.

'Brig, what are you going to do with it?' Sachs asked.

I glanced across the flickering flames of the fire. 'I'm going to get back into the cattle business,' I told him.

4

I took my leave the next morning after breakfast. I had plenty of supplies behind my saddle. Joel gave me two of his books to take along. I knew how much he prized them and promised to look after them.

'You take care of yourself, Brig,' he said. I realised then just how much I had come to like this serious young man. He was much like myself in what he wanted out of life. We both had dreams to fulfill, a lot of hills to climb, both in our different ways.

'I'll be seeing you soon,' I told him.

Leaving Seth and Jacob was the hardest part. We had hardly ever been apart since we'd been born. We had grown up together and had shared everything we had ever had. But we were fully grown now and we had always known that one day there would be a time when we would have to go our separate ways. I had never expected it to be me who would break away first. We said little, but words were never really needed between us. They wished me luck and I told them to watch out for me as I would soon be back. Sachs came over just before I rode out and put a brown hand on my knee.

'Good luck, boy. I hope you find what you're lookin' for.' He gave me a slow, wistful smile, his eyes suddenly far away. 'Hell, Brig, I wish I was as young as you an' just settin' out.'

'And I wish I knew as much about what's out there as you do,' I told him.

I rode out then, turning once to raise my arm to Joel, who stood watching me for some long time.

My horse was eager to be off, for he'd done little since we'd started to work the mine. He was well rested and it took some holding him back. I turned him up into the hills and soon the mine was far below, out of sight and sound, but not out of thoughts.

It was a warm day. As I rode higher the air became fresher, stirred by a faint breeze and soon I could smell the tang of the trees that grew on the upper slopes. A feeling of contentment came over me. It was silent up here. I could hear the buzzing of some insects, sometimes the song of a bird.

By noon I was well up in the higher slopes. I had left the sparse scrub and rock behind me. Where I rode now there was tall grass and great stands of towering green trees. There were numerous clear streams that twisted and bounded down the lush slopes. I rode through shadowed tunnels, through the intertwining branches of trees, where the sunlight filtered through in pale shimmering shafts of gold. Underfoot the earth was thick with leaf mould. I came across deep pools where fish swam in their dozens and it was by one of these that I stopped to rest.

I left my horse cropping the lush grass while I built a small fire and made coffee. I had bacon and flour, and while the coffee brewed I made myself some pancakes and fried some bacon. When I'd eaten I washed my utensils in the water and sat back to enjoy the beauty around me and to take a smoke.

I could have stayed there for the rest of the day, but I wanted to get on. Packing my gear I mounted up and set off.

I had earlier found out that there was a cattle-settlement some few days' ride over the hills and it was to this place that I was heading. My intention was to buy some good beef cattle and to drive them back to Hope, with the help of men I would hire. Back in Hope I expected to be able to sell the cattle at a good profit. It sounded an easy proposition but I didn't expect it to be that easy.

I was banking on a fair amount of good luck and the hope that nobody else got the idea and carried it through before I did. If I got my beef to Hope first I didn't see why I shouldn't sell it. There had been little in the way of fresh meat in the camp for months. Summer was drawing to a close and I figured that once winter set in there would be little that would get in or out of Hope. I realised that I was speculating but I also knew that if a man just sat back and never tried to do anything then he couldn't blame anybody but himself if he ended up with nothing. But I was young and had plenty of enthusiasm and I figured that if this didn't work out I could always try something else.

I camped that night under the stars. The night air was crisp and clear, the sky black and wide. Around me the hills lay silent and dark. I turned into my blankets early and was asleep soon after I lay down my head.

The next day passed in pretty much the same way yet I never once found myself getting bored or restless. There was so much to see, so much to store inside to remember. More than once I went out of my way to take a closer look at something.

After a second restful night I got up

in time to have breakfast and be in my saddle as the sun came up. It was a sight I've long remembered. The darkness slowly giving way to the day. The dawn sky going from black to grey to pink, then streaking with a dull red that flowed out over the hills around me. I rode slowly into the sunrise and watched the land come alive, glowing with a muted orange before the natural colours emerged into the hush of the dawn. It was a sight to see and made me thankful that I could see it.

About mid-morning I rode down a gentle slope, out of some trees, and saw before me a wide meadow of deep grass. A generous stream flowed across the land, bordered by trees and greenery. There were cattle too. Fat, healthy cattle. I rode by them, studying them closely. They were shorthorns and I realised that someone had some good stock here. Each beast bore a brand on its hip. It was the letter T in a circle; the Circle-T.

I rode on for almost an hour, keeping

the stream in sight, for I guessed that whoever owned the cattle would undoubtedly have some form of habitation near and it was bound to be close to the stream.

I saw it first through some trees. A small, neat house with a small barn close by and a couple of stout corrals. A smaller cabin stood beyond the barn. A number of horses were in one of the corrals. As I came out of the trees I could see a thin spiral of smoke coming from the stone chimney. I took my horse across the yard, which was hard-trodden earth long devoid of grass. I sat my saddle before the house, waiting to be asked before I stepped down as was the custom.

'Hello the house,' I called. 'Anyone home?'

I heard movement inside and the door opened. A tall, grey-haired man stepped out onto the covered porch that ran the length of the house. He came to the edge of the porch, shielding his eyes from the bright sun as he gazed up at me. He looked to be about fifty, a broad, handsome man who held himself tall and straight. There was something about him that spoke of strength, of solid character. His clothing was good, his appearance speaking of breeding that seemed somehow out of place with his surroundings.

'I was passing through,' I said. 'I saw your place and the cattle. I'm on the lookout for beef. Wondered if you were in a mind to trade.'

'We can talk better over a cup of coffee,' he said. 'Step down and come inside.'

I dismounted and tied my horse. Taking off my hat I followed the man inside. The interior was cooly comfortable. Whoever had built this house knew what he was doing. It was sturdy and larger inside than the exterior showed it to be. It was well furnished too. Rugs lay across the wooden floor and there were curtains at the windows. I detected the touch of a woman about the place. The vase of flowers on a small table, the shine and polish on everything.

I turned to face my host. 'I'm Brigham Tyler,' I said, holding out my hand.

'William Thorpe, Mr Tyler. Please sit down.'

We seated ourselves in big leather armchairs before the empty fireplace. I was feeling a little out of place in this room, conscious of being dusty from my ride and before I could stop myself I had touched a hand to my unshaven face. I felt William Thorpe's eyes on me, a smile on his lips as he said, 'Mr Tyler, would you do me the honour of dining with us?' He went on: 'We can talk then and I'm sure you'd welcome a chance to freshen up.'

I nodded. 'I could, sir, and I'm grateful for the offer. But I don't want to put you to any trouble.'

'You won't do that,' I heard someone say. I stood up, turning around as I did, and laid my eyes on Judith Thorpe for the first time.

'My daughter Judith,' Thorpe said. 'This is Mr Brigham Tyler. I've asked him to stay and eat with us.'

'You're more than welcome, Mr Tyler,' she said.

'Thank you, ma'am.' I must have looked pretty silly, the way I was staring at her, but it had been a long time since I'd seen a really pretty girl and Judith Thorpe would have taken the prize over any other.

She gave me a warm, bright smile, and said something about there being water out back if I wanted to wash. I followed her through into the kitchen, then outside to a neat bath-house. She brought me hot water and a towel, and William Thorpe came out with a razor so I could shave. And I had to admit that when I came out I felt a damn sight more human and presentable.

We sat down to the kind of meal I hadn't seen in a long time. There was roast beef, with potatoes and greens and thick gravy. It was followed by apple pie and fresh cream from their own cows. It was topped off by hot black coffee that tasted fresher than I thought possible. Thorpe must have sensed my hunger for such good food that he left the talk until after the meal.

'Miss Thorpe, I want to thank you for the best meal I've eaten for a long time.'

She was across the table from me and I saw her cheeks colour and she glanced quickly at her father. He was smiling, his eyes holding a kind of sparkle, and I wondered what I'd said.

'Judith has always maintained that my compliments about her cooking are said just for the sake of politeness. I've been telling her for some time that one day she would have some young man telling her the same and really meaning it.'

'All I can say is that I'm glad it was me,' I said.

Thorpe and I took our coffee back to the armchairs. He produced a box of cigars and we lit up. Judith was somewhere in the background, clearing the table, and my eyes were drawn to her as she came and went, joining in the conversation, filling our cups as they became empty. As I've said I don't consider myself a ladies man, but I know a woman when I see one, and there was something about this lovely girl that took and laid hold of me and wouldn't let go. It was more than physical, although she was of a shape that couldn't be ignored, what with her long dark hair and blue eyes that were bright and alive. Eyes that looked at a man with a boldness that was at times downright startling. She had long legs beneath her skirts and strongly curved hips. Her waist was small, but she filled out above it into full, proud breasts that pressed strongly against the bodice of her dress. I found that I was taking close note of these things, almost without realising it, and more than once I caught Judith gazing at me, and I averted my eyes for fear of offending her.

Shortly William Thorpe and I got down to the main reason for my visit. I told him of my plan to buy cattle and to sell them in Hope. Thorpe was a good listener and he let me have my say before he spoke.

'I admire your ambition, Mr Tyler. I never cease to wonder at the way boys grow into men so quickly in this country. Look at you. Even at your age you have your way planned out and I have a feeling you'll carry it through. You own part of a goldmine and now you plan to go into the cattle business.'

I drained my cup. 'From what I can see you've done pretty well yourself, sir. This place is as nice as I've seen anywhere. You've picked good graze-land. Plenty of water and grass. You're well protected come winter. I couldn't wish for a better place myself.'

He smiled 'May I call you Brigham?'

'I'd rather it was Brig. I haven't been called Brigham for a long time.'

'Brig it is then.' He reached out and picked up the coffee pot, refilling our cups. 'Now about cattle. I'm afraid I must disappoint you. My herd isn't for sale.'

'May I ask why, sir?'

'Those beeves out there are the start of what I hope will be a large herd in a few years. It's taken me some time to build up the beginning of a herd and it's my intention to breed from them. I hope you understand.'

'Of course, sir. It was just a notion.'

We talked for a time about cattle and Thorpe gave me some sound advice on what to look for when I went to do my buying. He also gave me the names of a couple of men I should visit when I reached my destination. I was to use his name for he was known and respected by the men he spoke of.

A while later Judith joined us and we talked of many things. I learned that Thorpe's father had been born in this country two weeks after his parents had arrived from England. I told them about Lancashire and of my early life there with my brothers and my father. Our mother had died shortly after I'd been born. I had never known her but I had heard my father talk of her. He had never really got over her death and had it not been for Seth and Jacob and myself he would have had little to live for. As it was he died in a pit explosion one night while he was working an extra shift, trying to earn extra money.

'So we decided to come to America,' I said. 'There was nothing at home and we'd heard all about the chances there were here, so we got aboard a ship and somehow we made it.'

'But you were only nine years old when you landed,' Judith said. 'How did you live? How did you . . . ' She broke off, her face suddenly flushing. 'I'm sorry,' she apologised. 'I didn't mean to pry.'

'I'm glad you find me interesting enough to ask,' I told her.

She smiled. 'I'll go and make some fresh coffee.'

Thorpe watched her go. 'She gets little enough company of her own age, Brig. I sometimes get the feeling I'm doing her harm keeping her out here, away from everything. But she is all I live for.'

'May I ask about Mrs Thorpe, sir?'

'She died when Judith was ten. That was ten years ago. A long time. We were in New England then. I had a farm my father had left me. I suppose we were what you would call extremely comfortable. But after Martha died I became restless. In the end I sold the farm and we moved here. We travelled the area for a year or two, until I found this place. It took time but the house was built and then I started to work towards the herd you saw.'

'You have a place to be proud of.'

'I think so, Brig.'

Thorpe invited me to stay the night and I was more than glad to. There was something about this place and the people that I liked. I hoped that I would be able to visit this place again. I liked William Thorpe. I could talk to him and found him easy to listen to. But I had to admit that the main reason I wanted to come back was Judith. I was finding that I couldn't get her out of my mind and what was more I found I didn't want to get her out of my mind. Just looking at her did things to me, stirring me in a way no girl had ever stirred me before.

We ate supper then sat drinking more coffee before a roaring log fire. Though the day had been warm, night brought a chill to the air. We talked for a long time. It was William Thorpe who excused himself first, saying that he had to be up early.

I wanted to see to my horse before I turned in. Judith brought me a lantern and I made my way over to the barn, leading my horse. I unsaddled him, gave him feed and water. On my way back to the house I saw a dark figure by the corral and I knew it was Judith.

'You have a beautiful country up here,' I said as I joined her.

She nodded. She was standing close to me and I could smell a faint perfume. The night breeze caught her dark hair and some of it drifted across my face. I could feel that stirring in me again and I knew that I was going to have to step careful.

'What's it like in a gold-camp, Brig?' Judith asked. 'May I call you Brig?'

'Rather that than Mr Tyler.'

She laughed softly, a sound as warm as a summer breeze. 'Then you must call me Judith.'

'I will. About Hope. Well all I can tell you is it's wild and noisy and dirty and violent.'

'It sounds exciting.'

'Maybe so but it is no place for a lady.'

She gazed at me with those beguiling eyes. 'Thank you for that.'

'May I walk you to the house, Judith?' Saying her name was strange to me. But not unpleasant.

'You may.' She reached out and took my arm. Her hand was slim and gentle on my arm but it did things to me that made me want to run up the nearest tree and yell.

We went inside and she fastened the

door. I followed her through the house to the room I was to use. I opened the door, then paused.

'Goodnight, Judith,' I said.

She raised her eyes to mine and we gazed at each other for a while.

'Goodnight, Brig,' she said finally.

I undressed and climbed into the bed that had been made up for me. I could hear movement beyond the wall where I lay and I realised it was coming from the room that Judith used. I listened for a while, then turned on my side and tried to sleep. I was well fed, secure, had little to worry me, yet I found I was restless, and sleep came hard that night.

5

After breakfast I saddled up my horse and prepared to carry on with my journey. I had already said goodbye to William Thorpe, for he had ridden out much earlier to do some tallying. I had made a firm promise to visit him on my return and I knew that I would always be welcome in his house.

I led my horse across to the house and tethered him. Judith came out before I could go inside. She held a neat, paper-wrapped package in her slim hands.

'I've made you up a few sandwiches,' she said.

I took them and put them in my saddlebags. Turning back to her I took off my hat and hoped I could find the right words.

'May I come to call on you, Judith?'

'Please do, Brig, I shall look out for you.'

I made to go, then on impulse I took her in my arms and I kissed her. And she responded in a way that took my breath away, pressing her soft mouth hard on my own, her arms holding me like she would never let go. Something told me I would never forget this girl and nothing would ever be able to stop me from coming back to her.

Finally I drew away from her and got onto my horse. I gathered rein and looked down at her. Judith smiled at me and I said, 'I'll be back.' She nodded gently and raised a hand as I turned my horse away. She stayed where she was, on the porch, and she was still there when my horse dipped us out of sight beyond a grassy ridge.

I rode like a man in a dream. I guess in a way I was dreaming, for it took a long time before I could accept what had happened. It made a difference. That girl back there had changed my life in a way that no other single thing had ever affected my life before. It took some grasping. But what made it so good was the fact that Judith plainly felt the same way about me. I felt that my life was a little more complete and that it would never be the same again.

I was even more determined to make good on my venture now. I knew that when I next visited the Thorpe ranch I would ask Judith to be my wife and I also knew that she would say yes. Maybe I was presuming a lot but sometimes a man gets a feeling and he knows that he is right. This was one of those feelings.

I rode all that day and nearly until noon of the next.

My way took me clear through the range of hills and down the far slopes into a wide and green valley. Scattered around the valley were a number of ranches and up towards the far end of the valley lay the small town that served the out-lying spreads.

Just before mid-day I rode along the single street of that small town and dismounted before the saloon. I was dry and a glass of beer would go down well. I gazed up and down the wide, dusty street before I went in. It was a nice town. Quiet, unhurried, the buildings neat and painted. It was an established town, this place called Tarrant. There was a stone-built jailhouse, a telegraph office, and a bank. I would be visiting there before I left, for William Thorpe had given me a letter of introduction to the bank's president.

First though I wanted that beer, so I went up the worn, sun-warped steps and into the saloon's cool interior. It was pretty well full but I found myself a place at the bar and ordered a beer when the barman came my way. 'New in town?' he asked and I nodded. 'Name's Joe Baily,' he added.

'Brig Tyler. Nice little town you've got.'

'We think so.' He put my beer before me. 'You on the lookout for a job?'

'Do I look that down-at-heel?' I tasted my beer. 'I'm in the market for some good beef,' I told Baily. 'Was up at William Thorpe's place the other day and he gave me a couple of names. George Dodd. Ben Choate. You know them?'

Baily nodded. 'You're in luck. That's George Dodd over there by the window,' he said and pointed.

I followed his finger. Thanking him I wandered across to where Dodd was sitting alone, nursing a beer. He was a big man, broad-shouldered. His thick hair and mustache were grey, his seamed face brown and full of character.

'Mr Dodd, may I have a few words with you?'

He glanced up at me. 'Do I know you, son?'

'No, sir. I'm Brig Tyler and I'm on the lookout for some beef. William Thorpe told me to look you up.'

'Bill did, eh? Sit down, son. How is Bill?'

'He's well, sir.'

Dodd seemed to be sizing me up. He took a gulp of his beer. He leaned back in his seat. 'You want to buy beef?'

'Yes, sir,' I said and I explained my plan to him. 'I want to get as much beef into Hope as I can before winter sets in.'

'You've got a good head on those big shoulders, boy,' Dodd said. 'Don't know why nobody's ever thought of doing what you intend. I wish you luck. You ride out to my place tomorrow and we'll look over some stock.'

'Thank you, sir. May I buy you another beer?'

Dodd grinned. 'I can see you're going to be a good businessman. Already softening me up.'

I stayed with Dodd for over an hour. When I left the saloon I made my way down to the bank and went inside. It was typical of most banks I'd been in. It smelled of dusty ledgers, ink, and I swear it smelled of money too.

There was nobody in the place save for a skinny, pale young man behind the counter. He watched me as I crossed the hardwood floor and I could swear that he imagined I'd come to hold the place up. I suppose I did look somewhat down-at-heel, with my dusty clothing and run-over boots. I hadn't shaved since I'd left the Thorpe place. And as well as my holstered handgun I was carrying my rifle in my left hand, a habit I had recently acquired.

'I'd like to see the boss man,' I told the pale-faced man.

He gave me a look up and down. By now he'd decided I wasn't out to rob him but that didn't make him any more polite.

'I'm sure whatever your business, I can accommodate you,' he said and I took a dislike to him straightaway. His voice was thin and pale, just like he looked.

I lay my rifle on his polished counter and cuffed my stained hat back. 'Now look, sonny,' I said quietly, 'I asked nice and polite. I want to think you didn't understand, so I'll ask again. I'd like to have a word with the president. Not the hired hand. The boss. Now you go and ask him if he'll see me and give him this letter.' I placed William Thorpe's letter on the counter. 'Light out, boy, else I'm liable to get upset.'

He took the letter and made his way over to the door that plainly led to the office of the bank's president. The name on the door read: George Q. Heath. Paleface went in and closed the door and I could hear the low murmur of voices. It wasn't long before the door opened and Paleface came out.

'Mr Heath will see you now, Mr Tyler,' he said.

I went past him and into the office. The door shut gently behind me.

Heath's office was all carpet and oak panels. A big oak desk took up a lot of room and the man behind it took up a fair piece himself. Heath, George Q. was fat and pink and bald. But he looked like a man who knew his job and where money was concerned I was sure he was no man's fool.

'Please take a seat, Mr Tyler,' Heath said. He took my hand as I sat down and his grip was surprisingly firm. 'How is Bill Thorpe?'

'He's well, sir.'

'And that pretty daughter of his?'

I took off my hat. 'She is well too.'

'Good. Now, Mr Tyler, I'm sure you didn't come here to indulge in idle chit-chat. Bill's letter speaks highly of you and he says you have ambition. How can I help you?'

I took my pouch of gold out of my shirt where I'd been carrying it since I'd arrived in town. It was no featherweight and I was glad to be rid of it. I put it on Heath's desk.

'I'd like to put this in your keeping. Open an account.'

Heath inspected the gold. 'Looks to be high grade,' he said. 'You any idea how much there is here?'

'One of my partners knows something about these things. He said that bag should fetch around eight thousand, give or take a few dollars.'

'I'll have the assay office take a look. Be able to tell you in the morning just what it is worth but I don't think you'll be far wrong.'

He put the bag aside and got up, crossing over to a small table that held cut-glass decanters and heavy glasses. He brought me a tumbler of what turned out to be some very fine mellow brandy.

'What are your plans, Mr Tyler?'

I outlined my idea and he listened interestedly.

'You've chosen a good man to deal with in George Dodd. He'll treat you fair.'

'That's all I want from any man,' I said.

'You got anywhere for the night?'

'Not yet,' I told him.

'Try the Tarrant House. It's clean and comfortable. Might cost a little more but it is worth it.'

I nodded, wondering if my cash money would run to a place like the Tarrant House. Heath must have seen my thoughts in my face. He gave a knowing little smile.

'You need any money to get you by?' he asked.

'Well, I guess I could use a few dollars.'

Heath wrote something on a sheet of notepaper and handed it to me. 'We'll credit it to your account.'

'Grateful, Mr Heath,' I said.

'That's what we're here for,' he said.

We talked for a little time. He was interested to hear about the doings up at Hope. I reckoned it was that he was a banker and anything to do with money was interesting to him. Before I left we made arrangements for me to call in the next day.

On the way out I passed over Heath's note to the Paleface. He read it, then opened his cash drawer and began counting out a pile of banknotes. He stopped when he reached two hundred dollars. I hadn't realised just how much Heath had put me down for. I'd never had that much money in my hand before but I didn't let it worry me none. I'd always taken things as they come and a change for the better was not to be sneezed at.

I left the bank and collected my horse. I walked him down to the livery and left him in the hands of the old man who ran the place, with instructions to look after him well. Then I took me back up the street and called in at the barber shop for a shave and a trim.

On my way up to the hotel I passed a hardware store and I turned about and went inside. The feller inside became real helpful when I told him what I was after. I came out with a wrapped parcel under my arm that contained a couple of pairs of new Levi's, a couple of new shirts, new socks, and a pair of new, hand-stitched boots.

The Tarrant House was big and expensive, by Western standards. The clerk at the back of the desk was just about as snotty as the one in the bank. I don't think he was too happy about my trailing my dirty boots across his plush carpet. He didn't seem too keen on giving me a room until I told him who had sent me over. I got a nice room that overlooked the street and it had its own bathroom attached. That took some swallowing, I can tell, but I figured I might as well enjoy what I was paying for. I sent down to have the bath filled, then spent a good hour soaking off the trail dirt.

I lazed around until it got dark, then put on my new clothes and boots and went out to eat. I found a quiet little eating house a few doors down from the hotel and I had a good meal, finishing off with a pot of hot coffee.

Later I made my way to the saloon. The evening trade was starting to pick up and it was a few minutes before I was able to have a word with the barman, Joe Baily. I ordered a beer, then told him I was on the lookout for a couple of good cowhands.

'Your luck's in again,' he said. He pointed to a couple of men sitting at a table by one of the saloon's big windows. 'They came in this afternoon. Both of 'em looking for work.'

'They any good?'

Baily nodded. 'I known 'em both for some time. Good workers. They know cows and they stay on the job.'

I tasted my beer. 'I'll go and see what they think of me.'

'The stocky one with the mustache is Joe Crown,' Baily said. 'Other one is Lew Riley.'

I took my beer and made my way across to where the two men were seated. It was plain to see that they were cowhands, for their clothing spoke of their trade. Each man wore high-heeled boots, Crown's had big Mexican spurs afixed, though he'd had the sharp tips filed off the wheels. He was also wearing tough leather chaps that looked as if they had seen a lot of work. Both men were armed. Crown wore his handgun on his right hip, fairly low. Lew Riley, lean and dark, had his gun on his left side, high up, the butt forward for a crossdraw.

I reached their table. Crown saw me first and I saw his eyes flick over me fast. He was a man who was on the alert all the time. Before I spoke, I knew he had me sized up.

'Heard you were looking for work,' I said. 'I'm hiring.'

Crown leaned back in his chair. 'Little young, aren't you?' he asked. There was no sarcasm in his voice. He was simply stating a fact and waiting for an answer.

I tipped back my hat. 'Way I see it, a dollar bill is the same whether it comes from a boy or a ninety-year old man.'

Crown grinned easily. 'I guess you are right. You better sit and tell us what you want.'

I took an empty chair. They told me their names and I nodded. 'I'm Brig Tyler. Been working over to Hope. Me and my brothers and two partners have a mine going.'

'Any luck?' Riley asked.

I smiled. 'Fair.'

'I hope you ain't lookin' for miners,' Crown said.

'No. I want men who can work

cattle.' I told them my scheme and offered them good money. 'I'm going over to George Dodd's spread in the morning to look over some beef so I'd like to get settled before I turn in.'

'Lew?' Crown glanced at his partner.

'He's offerin' fair wages.'

Crown inclined his head. 'Looks like you got yourself a couple of hands,' he said.

We shook hands. I took them over to the bar and bought them a beer.

'You any kin to the feller that shot Cole Prentise over at Hope?' Crown asked.

'My brother Jacob,' I said. 'News gets around fast.'

Crown smiled. 'You'd be surprised. We heard about it two days after it happened.' He glanced at me. 'We heard there was a feller had a run-in with Red Karver and come out best. That was over to Hope as well. Seems I recall the name was Tyler in that scrape too.'

'My other brother Seth and me.

Karver figured he wanted our mine but we changed his mind for him.'

'You know, Joe,' Riley said, 'I'm glad we're working for this feller and not working against him.'

Crown drained his beer glass. 'Me too,' he said but I doubted if he was really bothered. From what I could see Joe Crown was a man who could look out for himself and I couldn't see him backing down from any man. And that went for Riley as well.

We talked for a while, then I left them. I wanted an early night. Returning to the hotel I went up to my room and turned in. I slept well and woke just as dawn began to streak the sky. I washed and dressed, put on my gunbelt. I went down and made my way along to the eating house. Crown and Riley were already there and I joined them for breakfast.

I walked down to the bank after breakfast. Heath had an account-book filled out in my name, with credit to the amount of $8,200.

'Your gold assayed out at $8,400,' he told me. 'I've deducted the two hundred you took yesterday.'

Those figures looked mighty comforting to me. I wondered just what that amount would look like after I'd made my cattle deal with the miners at Hope. I might make myself a pile. Then again I might end up with nothing.

From the bank I went to the store and had a big order of provisions made up. I also took some extra boxes of rifle and pistol shells. While I was there I spotted some made-up dresses on a rack and I went across and chose one that I liked the look of, took it over to the storekeeper.

'You know Judith Thorpe?' I asked him.

'I do. Why?'

'You think this will fit her?'

He grinned. 'I'd better ask my wife.' He called her out and told her what I needed to know. She took one look at the dress and nodded her head approvingly.

While the dress was being wrapped I picked out a box of good cigars for William Thorpe. I paid for everything and went down to the livery. Crown and Riley were waiting for me. I saddled up, put the dress and cigars in my saddlebags. The foodstuff was distributed between the three of us and I split up the boxes of shells three ways.

'I hope we don't have to use these,' I said, 'but if we run into any trouble I've only one rule — if the other feller is out for trouble, shoot first and we'll hold the inquest later.'

We mounted up and rode out of town. Crown knew the way to Dodd's ranch so he led the way. The day was fine and sunny. We rode steadily, without hurry. It took almost three hours to reach Dodd's big Double-D spread. We crossed the dusty yard and reined in before the sprawling house. Dodd was a bachelor and his spread was an all-male preserve. Somehow it showed. The place was well kept but it was obvious that it lacked a woman's hand.

Obvious too was the fact that Dodd did everything on a big scale. His barns and stables, his maze of corrals and cattle-pens, all were big, sturdily built to last a lifetime and maybe longer.

Dodd himself came across from one of the corrals where a spot of horse-breaking was going on. Today he was dressed for work in dusty, stained Levis and faded shirt, a battered hat tipped to the back of his head.

'Glad you could make it, Mr. Tyler,' he said. 'I'll fetch my horse and we'll go take a look at some beef.' He glanced at Crown and Riley. 'Hello, Jim. How are you, Lew?'

'Fine, George,' Crown said.

'You hired these boys?' Dodd asked.

'Last night.'

'You couldn't have chosen better,' he said. He crossed to a hitch-rail and climbed onto a big black.

He led out of the yard and across country at a steady pace. We rode for about twenty minutes, eventually coming to a shallow green basin that held a bunch of about 250 head. We rode in amongst them. I ran my eye over them. They were all full-grown beasts but they weren't old. There was some good meat on them. They were all healthy too. Well fed and watered.

'We've been trimming the herd for the winter,' Dodd told me. 'By next year this bunch will be too far gone for the first drives. The Eastern markets like young stuff. It's not worth my while keeping these. We use a lot for our own meat, sell some in town. You can have as many of these as you want.'

'What's your price?' I asked.

Dodd smiled dryly. 'I can see you're bound to get on.'

He started off by asking $22.50 a head. I didn't figure on paying him that much. I'd already decided on my figure and I wasn't going to pay a cent over it. We haggled some but Dodd saw that I wasn't too keen on anything above the price I'd quoted and finally we agreed. I would take the 250 head at twenty dollars a head. We rode back to the house and Dodd made out a bill of sale and signed it. He would ride into town with us and we would settle the deal at the bank.

It was just after noon when we got the herd on the move. The beeves, fed and rested, caused us no trouble and we made good time, reaching Tarrant in the late afternoon. Crown and Riley stayed with the herd while I rode in with Dodd. We went to the bank and closed our deal. I was anxious to be on my way before dark and before I left Dodd said that if I wanted more cattle I knew where to find him.

I rejoined Crown and Riley and we got the herd moving, taking it round Tarrant. The two men knew their job well and I had little to do save working along with them. The trail was fairly level here and we had little trouble. We pushed the herd until dark and then we got them bedded down before we made camp for the night.

Riley assumed the position of cook without being told or asking. When we sat down to eat I found that he was more than fair at the job. We had beans and pancakes and bacon. And his coffee was of the kind that a man can get to like.

I learned a little of what Crown and Riley had done since they had teamed up before the war. Cattle had been their trade all along, save for a couple of forays into beaver-trapping and buffalo-hunting. During the war they had worked for the Union Army, supplying beef. The work had been hard and often dangerous, but, as Crown told me, that was the cattle business all the time, in war and peace. It was hard and dangerous any way a man wanted to look at it but it was a job he wouldn't have exchanged for any you could mention.

We talked and drank Riley's coffee until late. We had decided to run a night-guard on the herd and I had fallen for the first turn. I mounted up and rode out to where the herd was.

The night was clear and the air was chilly. I was glad of my heavy sheep-skin coat. I'd had it for a couple of years now and it had served me through two cold winters. As I circled the quiet herd I wondered what this coming winter would bring for me. I could come out of it a rich man. I could come out worse off than before. I thought of Seth and Jacob, of Joel, of old Sachs. I thought too of men like Red Karver and his like, wondering what might come my way from them. But most of all I thought of Judith and the fact that I would soon be seeing her again.

6

The really hard work came once we started pushing the herd up into the hills. As we got higher the way became much more difficult. We managed but our pace was cut down to a slow walk. I took to riding on ahead, scouting out the way in front. It helped for I was able to seek out the best way for us to push the herd. On the second day, around midmorning, the sky darkened over and shortly after it brought cold rain. We pulled on our slickers and carried on. The beeves were none too pleased about the rain and their mournful sounds of protest could be heard above the hissing downpour.

Night of the second day found us making camp in the slight shelter of a rocky overhang. We sat around the flickering cookfire and drank coffee. The air was penetrating, the rain unceasing. We were wet and cold and in no mood for idle talk. Even Riley's cooking seemed to have suffered. His beans and bacon had been near to tasteless. As we huddled there, each man silently hanging on to his own thoughts, I wondered how long the rain would last. The ground was already sodden, the soil turned to sticky, clinging mud. Water cascaded down the hill slopes, making the way that much more treacherous. Up to now we had got by without mishap. I was hoping it would continue that way.

Riley was on first watch. When he had gone I pulled my blanket around me and tried to sleep. For a time I lay listening to the rain, the spitting, cracking of the fire. Then I must have drifted off, for the next thing I knew I was being wakened roughly, and Crown's voice, low and hushed, was warning me to keep quiet.

'What's wrong?' I asked.

Crown's face was highlighted by the fire's flickering glow. 'We seem to have company,' he said. 'Only they appear to be more interested in the herd than us.'

I got out of my blanket and reached for my rifle, checking the action. Crown moved off, heading away from the fire, into the darkness and I followed him close. It was still raining, though now it had slackened off into a slow drizzle. I buttoned my thick jacket up around my neck, turning the collar up.

The herd was in a shallow, natural basin. It formed a long, wide oval, and had been ideal for our purpose. It had meant that whoever was on watch would be able to see the entire herd in one look.

Crown led me to where Riley was crouched beside a large rock, his hat pulled low over his eyes, shoulders hunched against the cold. He glanced round as we joined him. 'I counted eight of them,' he said, pointing to the far side of the basin.

As I looked, and saw the eight mounted riders, two more appeared out of the night. They were plainly outlined on the rim of the basin. It looked to me as if they were either fools or very confident of their ability to take the herd without trouble. Well, I was afraid they were going to be somewhat upset this night.

'We'd better spread,' I said. 'Soon as they move for the herd I'll give them one warning, then open fire if they don't take heed.'

Crown nodded. Riley gave me a tight smile. Then they moved away from me, each going in a different direction.

Then, it was a matter of waiting. Our visitors seemed to be having some kind of debate. I never did find out just what it was they were talking about.

Of a sudden they started moving, urging their horses down the slope of the basin. I let them get so far down, then I stood up, my rifle ready.

'All right, gents, that's far enough. Back off and keep going. This herd's spoken for. You've had your warning, take it. I start shooting in a minute.'

My words must have reached them

for every man jerked his horse to a stop. But they didn't back off. I heard a man laugh. It was a deep, heavy laugh, and it was followed by the wicked crack of a rifle. I saw a stab of orange flame, then heard the bullet smack against the rock close by my right side. I dropped to the ground, jerking my rifle up and loosed off a shot at the bunched riders.

And then the night opened up with gunfire, stabs of flame flickering, the whip-crack sounds of a dozen rifles. Crown and Riley laid down a deadly stream of fire from either side of me, and along with my own fire, we cut a bloody swathe through the ranks of the night-riders.

They returned our fire but they did little harm. I think we had taken them off guard. I don't think they had been expecting such resistance.

I felt my rifle click on an empty chamber. Drawing into the lee of my protecting rock I thumbed fresh loads into the breech. But before I could rejoin the fight it was all over.

The rifle fire from across the basin slackened, then ceased. Hooves pounded the wet earth as the bunch of raiders rode off. Silence returned, only broken by the bawling of the unsettled herd. It was only later that I realised we had been firing over the heads of the herd. Why they didn't stampede I'll never know.

I stood up, sleeving mud from my face. Crown came out of the gloom, his face creased in a smile.

'Man, did we shake 'em up.' He thumbed fresh loads into his rifle. 'You hurt?'

I shook my head. 'Only wet.'

Riley rejoined us. He had a slight cut on his left cheek, caused by a flying stone chip.

'That took the edge off a dull evening,' he said.

'Any idea who they might be?' I asked.

'Most probably the Reevers.'

'Who are they?'

Crown hunched his shoulders deeper

into his coat. 'Real bad hombres. Jack and Ollie. Been around this part of the country for a long time. They'll do most anything if it'll show a profit. Mostly though they concentrate on cattle. Rustling, brand-changing. You name it, they'll do it.'

'You think they'll try again?' I asked.

Riley nodded. 'They'll try. Only next time it'll be in daylight and they won't do any sneaking about. They'll come at us like a bat out of hell.'

'We'd better get some sleep,' I said, ''cause it appears that tomorrow might be a busy day.'

7

The rain ceased just before dawn and with full light the sky showed clear and blue. It looked as if it was going to be a good day, as far as the weather was concerned at least.

We had a quick breakfast, broke camp, and got the herd on the move. Our job was made more difficult now because we had to be on the lookout for any signs of our night-visitors, as well as carrying out the normal tasks that went with driving the herd.

The land around us was dotted fairly heavily with trees and brush, and it was uneven land, given to much rising and falling, holding many hollows and shallow ravines. It was terrain that strongly suited the ambusher for it could hide an army from the sight of anyone passing by. It gave us some worry and I think we were thankful when the something we were waiting for actually happened.

It was close on noon. The sun was up and it was hot. We had halted the herd by a shallow pool to let them drink while we had a smoke. We might have been resting, but we were certainly not relaxed and though we were casual in our appearance we were fully ready when a bunch of seven riders broke out of a stand of trees a few hundred yards from us.

They rode our way slowly. Every one of them was armed with a rifle and had handguns on their hips. From what I could make of them they were a rough, hard crew. A couple of them sported bandages. It looked like we had scored a few hits last night.

I glanced over at Crown and Riley. They hadn't moved yet but I knew they were ready to. I eased my horse over to them. Crown glanced at me.

'It's the Reevers,' he said. 'Jack is the thin one with the beard. The big feller with the green shirt is Ollie.'

I looked towards the drinking herd. Everything I had was in that herd. I wasn't going to give it up to anyone.

'Ever see a cavalry charge?' I asked.

Riley chuckled. 'No but I've always fancied being in one.'

'Then let's ride,' I said and I gigged my horse forward with a yell, taking myself towards the advancing Reever bunch. Behind me Crown and Riley did the same.

I jammed the butt of my rifle against my hip and as soon as I was in range I opened up. My first shot took a thick-set, one-eyed man clear out of his saddle, dumping him face down in the dirt. I kept firing and close by I could hear the sounds of the rifles belonging to Crown and Riley.

A second man left his saddle and at that point the Reever bunch broke up, going every direction except up. Guns started going off, bullets coming close. I drew rein and steadied my aim on Ollie Reever. I could have put him down but my attention was distracted by Crown who suddenly toppled out of his saddle and sprawled face down on the ground.

I wheeled my horse over towards him. Another rider was heading that way. It was the man who had shot Crown. He was a burly, scar-faced individual and it looked as if he were intent on making sure that Crown was dead.

I jammed my rifle into its sheath and got my handgun out and then Scar was before me and he saw me. He swung his rifle at me, levelling it, and I put a bullet in him fast, saw him buckle at the waist, surprise on his face. His mouth worked in a wordless yell. He pushed himself upright again and tried to lift his rifle again. I was close by then and I shot him again, the bullet slamming him out of the saddle. He lit on his face, then flopped over onto his back, his legs kicking for a minute before he died, and I thought he was mean enough to get up and keep coming.

A wild yell brought my head up. The

raiders were on the run and it was Riley making the noise. He was up in his stirrups, waving his hat at them.

I rode over to Crown and got down. He looked up at me and made to grin. His face was pale and shiny with sweat. He'd been shot through the fleshy part of the upper arm. There was a lot of blood, both back and front of the wound, and I took this to mean that the bullet had gone right through.

'How you feeling?' I asked.

He ran his tongue over his lips. 'Thirsty,' he said. 'And I hurt.'

'We'll get you fixed up,' I said. Riley was heading our way. 'Figure you'll be able to ride?'

'Well I ain't stayin' here.'

'I'll get you some water. Then we'll get you bandaged up.'

Riley bent over Crown for a minute. He opened Crown's shirt. 'Ain't too bad,' he said matter-of-factly.

I gave Crown my canteen. He drank deeply. 'The hell it ain't bad,' he said. 'They done shot my drinking arm.

102

Don't taste the same out of the left hand.'

Riley sat back, tipping his hat back from his face. 'See, he ain't bad hurt.'

We cleaned Crown's arm and got him wrapped up and on his horse. He insisted on helping with the herd and as much as I wanted him to rest I was glad of his help.

As we got the herd on the move we kept our eyes skinned in case the Reevers came back. I didn't think they would but we didn't figure to take any chances.

We left the three dead Reever men where they lay. I would have liked to have buried them but with the rest of the bunch nearby I figured it was wiser to move on. The dead men would have to lie until their friends came for them.

We pushed the herd as fast as we could and despite the rough terrain we made good time. By nightfall we were well clear of the area where the fight had taken place. I dropped back a number of times to check the backtrail.

Each time I came back with the news that we were not being followed. If I had been one of the Reevers, I would have given up by this time. It had already cost more than it was worth. There would be other cattle but dead men were gone forever, and bullets have no preference. They can kill a leader just as surely as they can kill one of his followers.

Riley found us a handy box-canyon for the night. We pushed the herd in and built a brush fence across the width of the canyon.

I made a fire at the mouth of the canyon, where we could sit with our backs to the high rock wall. While Crown put some coffee on I got the horses unsaddled. Riley took his rifle and went off some way to keep watch.

It was clear and cool after the heat of the day. Stars began to appear. The dark bulk of the hills lay behind us, in front the land fell away in a series of ridges and slopes. Down there, in amongst the trees and rocks, was the way we had come today. There was no regular trail and we had made our own. Tomorrow we would have to push the herd across even higher slopes, through thick stands of tall trees and heavy brush. One way or another we were going to earn our money.

Crown wanted to take his regular turn on watch, but Riley and I were both against the idea. After a lot of grumbling Crown turned into his blankets and lay down. His wound had left him weak, though he never would have said so and he was more tired than he showed. Once he was down he slept the night through, though when I came off my watch at dawn he was up and preparing breakfast.

'How you feeling?' I asked.

'Hungry.' He passed me a mug of coffee. 'Arm's stiff but I'll manage.'

Riley came back from getting the horses ready. We sat down and ate breakfast. After we had finished the coffee we broke camp, removed the brush-barrier, and drove the herd out of the canyon, turning them up onto the rising slopes.

Before we had been moving for two hours the way became even more difficult than I had imagined. The hill slopes were steep and trees and rocks and heavy brush made the going rough. To make things worse the sun came out with a vengeance, the heat adding to our discomfort. More than once we had to turn the herd away from some impassable obstruction and try to find a safer way round. It made the going slow and as the morning dragged by I realised that we were not going to make much distance until we reached easier ground.

The rest of that day saw us over the farthermost ridge and onto fairly level terrain. We were still in heavily-wooded country but it was a sight better than the rugged slopes we had come over, and it gave us time to relax.

Darkness was falling as we trailed the weary herd down a long, green slope that led into a grassy meadow. I could see a stream cutting its way across the meadow. We turned the herd that way and once the beeves got the scent they needed little coaxing.

Again we made camp, ate, took turns at watching the herd. With another dawn it was breakfast, break camp and then back to pushing the herd on towards Hope.

Late in the afternoon we came within sight of the Thorpe spread and I felt my spirits lift at the thought of seeing Judith again. I remembered, too, what I had set myself to ask her and for a moment I wondered if maybe I was taking too much for granted. Then I thought again and I knew I wasn't.

We drove the herd onto Thorpe range and watched them settle contentedly. Those beeves were as weary as we were and they wouldn't be doing any wandering.

'We'll sleep sound tonight, boys,' I told Crown and Riley as we rode in on the Thorpe ranch. 'These are nice people.'

'This girl of yours,' Crown asked, 'can she cook?'

I grinned at him through my stubble. 'Like you never tasted food before.'

'No wonder he's so much in a hurry to get there,' Riley said.

The house door flew open as we reined in and Judith came running out, her eyes bright, cheeks flushed. I came down out of my saddle and she was in my arms as my feet touched the ground. I kissed her hard and it was a moment in my life I knew I'd never forget. She held me like she was never going to let go.

'I didn't think you were coming back,' she said.

'Now don't tell me you really thought that,' I told her.

She smiled, shook her head. 'No. Not really. But I thought you might meet someone else. Maybe a prettier girl.'

'There's no such girl,' I said and I meant it.

I took her across to meet Crown and Riley. They were standing by their horses, trying to look as though they were minding their own business.

'Boys, this is Miss Judith Thorpe.' They took off their hats like they were real gentlemen and I knew that if I made one joke about it they would lay me out fast. 'Judith, this is Joe Crown and Lew Riley.'

'Ma'am, it's an honour,' Crown said. 'I can see now why Brig never stops talking about you.'

Riley only nodded, his face wreathed in a fixed smile.

I saw William Thorpe come out of the house and I went across to greet him. 'I'm taking you up on your offer of hospitality, sir.'

'You and your men are more than welcome,' he said. 'How did your trip go?'

'Very well, sir,' I told him.

'Tell you what, Brig. You and your men can get cleaned up and then we'll have supper and you can tell me all about it.'

The offer of supper was just what we

needed, and after bathing and shaving and changing into clean shirts, Crown and Riley and I sat down to one of Judith's welcome meals. We were hungry men and we did Judith proud, for there was nothing left on the table by the time we'd done.

'My goodness, don't you men eat while you're on the trail?' Judith asked.

Crown glanced at her, smiling. 'Yes, ma'am, we eat. But bacon and beans soon lose their flavour. If we could eat like we just have I don't think we'd have a thing to complain about.'

Judith refilled his coffee cup. 'Why thank you, Mr Crown.'

A little later I sat by the fire with William Thorpe. Crown and Riley were in the kitchen helping Judith with the washing up. They'd insisted on giving her help.

'Those are good men, Brig. The type who'll stick with you no matter what.'

'I know, sir. They've already proved their loyalty.'

'The Reevers?'

'Yes. Have you had any trouble from them?'

He shook his head. 'I've known they frequent these hills. People are always warning me about them but I've had no contact with them so far.'

'I hope you never do.'

Thorpe smiled. 'I'm prepared for most emergencies, Brig, so don't worry about me.'

I heard Judith's laughter from the kitchen and I was reminded of the matter I had to put to Thorpe before too long. There was no use in holding back I knew and I wasn't one for hesitating when it was time for speaking up.

'Sir, I have something I wish to say to you.'

Thorpe glanced at me steadily. 'What is it, Brig?'

'Sir, I want to marry Judith and I'd like your permission.'

Thorpe smiled gently, leaning back in his armchair. 'Have you asked her yet?' he inquired.

'Not yet, sir. I thought it right to speak to you first.' I hesitated. 'Sir, I love Judith and I want more than anything else I've ever wanted to marry her. I know I haven't known her long but I don't think that makes much difference. If I wasn't sure I would not have spoken up.'

'I know that, Brig, and I know you mean what you say. You go and ask her. If she'll have you, then you both have my blessing.'

I stood up. 'Thank you, sir. I can promise you that I'll look after her. She'll not want for anything.'

I made my way to the kitchen. Judith was just finishing tying a fresh bandage round Crown's arm. Riley sat across the table eating pie and drinking hot coffee. They glanced up as I appeared in the door.

'Brig, we may quit workin' for you and sign on here,' Riley grinned.

I said, 'You'll soon work off all that apple pie when we start for Hope.

Crown buttoned his shirt. 'Brig, why

don't you take this girl for a walk. She's done enough work for one night.'

'That's what I came for.'

I opened the kitchen door and followed Judith outside. The night was chill and bright with stars. We walked around to the front of the house and wandered off a small way. Wind blew softly through the trees and hissed through the grass. We hardly spoke as we walked.

'I like Joe and Lew,' Judith said after a while.

'They're good men,' I answered. 'I'd have been in real trouble if they hadn't have been with me this trip.'

Judith stopped suddenly, turning, her face pale in the starlight. 'Oh, Brig, you could have been killed,' she said, and the concern in her voice was strong.

'No chance of that,' I said. 'Not when I had you to come back to.'

She smiled then and I saw she was blushing.

'Judith, I had a talk with your father just now about something important.

113

Now I have something to ask you.'

She faced me, her eyes on me. 'Yes, Brig.'

For a moment I was speechless. Suppose she said no when I asked her. What would I do? But I knew she wouldn't say no and I wondered why I was hesitating.

'Judith, I love you and I want you to be my wife. Will you?'

She stood silent for a moment, her eyes big and wide. Then she came to me, put her arms around me. 'Yes, Brig. Oh, yes.'

I kissed her, kissed like I'd never kissed a girl before. We stayed there in the starry darkness, unmindful of the cold, oblivious of everything except each other and the strange excitement of this moment. I could feel a gentle trembling from Judith's close-pressed body and I became acutely aware of her firm, womanly contours as she stirred gently against me.

'I think we'd better go back in,' I said a little while later, 'else they'll be sending a search-party for us.'

She laughed softly. 'I don't care. Oh, Brig, I'm so happy.'

'And me,' I said.

We went on back up to the house. William Thorpe was in the kitchen with Crown and Riley. When we gave them our news Thorpe took us all into the house and poured glasses of brandy for us all. We stayed up late, talking and laughing, but I took little of it in. My eyes were for Judith and I was telling myself how lucky I was and wondering what the future held in store for us.

8

We stayed over at Circle-T for another day. It gave the herd a rest and it gave us one as well. It also gave me some more time with Judith and we put it to good use, planning for our marriage. I gave Judith the dress I'd bought for her and she was well pleased with it, wearing it that day.

That evening Judith gave us a fine meal before we turned in. I had decided on an early start. I wanted to get the herd to Hope as soon as possible. Once I had it off my hands I could start making plans for Judith and myself. There was much to do in the near future and I was eager to get started on it.

Before I turned in I took Judith for a walk beyond the house. We talked of our future. I told her my ambitions and she listened and encouraged me and just to have her there, to have her hear my plans, made them that much more exciting. I saw little that could stop me from putting them through.

We left the wedding-date open, not wanting to pin ourselves down for a few months yet. I needed time to get my cattle dealing on a firm footing. It would mean a lot of work, with little time to spare. But I didn't want to put things off for too long and I knew Judith didn't.

Come morning we ate breakfast and saddled up. We said our good-byes and I was loathe to leave Judith, but I consoled myself with the thought that I would be seeing her again soon.

Riding out to the herd we got it on the move, driving it easily across Circle-T range, and onto the downward slope of the hills. We had two days of driving ahead of us. The way was unmarked. As with the first part of our trip, we were going to have to blaze our own trail. It took us some time. We came upon numerous rough-spots and more than once we had to push the herd back the way we had come until we found an easier route. Twice on the first day it rained. It was the cold, icy rain of the high country and despite our slickers we got soaked. Luckily it stopped before nightfall so we were able to make camp in comparative comfort, building ourselves a good fire to dry our damp clothes.

The second day was worse than the first. Late in the afternoon we pushed the herd out of the timberline, onto the rocky lower slopes of the hills. There was a lot of tricky ground before us now. Long slopes of loose shale, crumbling ledges and sheer drops. There were jumbled falls of huge boulders, choked with brush, and here and everywhere there were countless holes and crevices to watch out for. The sun was out and it was hot and dry and dusty. Most of the time we were riding in a thick, misty cloud that clogged the mouth and nose, irritating the throat and making the eyes smart.

We coaxed and coddled that herd down those slopes, near enough carrying them over the rougher spots, dragging them out of trouble on the end of a rope more than once. And when finally we got them to the bottom we had only lost three out of the entire herd.

We were filthy, tired, sweat-soaked. Our eyes stung, our throats were swollen from eating dust. Our arms ached from working horses and ropes. We wanted baths, food, and sleep. But we had got the herd over those hills at the cost of only three lost steers.

Darkness was closing around us fast as we drove the herd across ground that was easy after what we had just come over. We were close on the mine now and it was my intention to bed the herd nearby for the night.

I hadn't expected to get too close without being spotted. I knew my brothers too well for that. Sachs and Joel as well. I was not disappointed, for as we pushed the weary herd up the long slope that faced onto the mine area I saw a rider approaching us.

It was Jacob. He rode straight to me, his face split by a wide grin.

'Damnit, Brig, it looks like you did it,' he said.

'I said I would.'

He sat for a moment looking the cattle over. 'They'll go wild in Hope when they see you bring this lot in,' he said.

'Wild enough to buy?' I asked.

Jacob laughed. 'God, yes. I figure they'll make you mayor.'

'Mayor of Hope?'

'Yeah. Things have been happening. A town council has been formed. Seems like they're trying to bring Hope to heel, get things organised. There's talk of a marshal being elected.'

'You think they'll get anyone to stand for that job?'

'They already have one candidate.' Jacob rubbed his chin. 'Seth.'

I wasn't overly surprised. Of the three of us Seth was the most civic-minded.

He understood the need for law and order better than either Jacob or I. He knew it had to be brought to the wild places like Hope, for if it wasn't they would simply burn themselves out and end up either as ghost-towns or kill-crazy hellholes. If Seth did get the job he'd make a go of it, that I knew. He had the patience and tolerance that any good lawman needed. He also had enough of the hard stuff in him to take on any odds but he also knew when to stop and draw the line.

Jacob gave us a hand to settle the herd before I rode into camp with him. Crown and Riley stayed with the herd. I would relieve them later but right now I wanted to see Seth and Joel and Sachs.

Supper was being cooked as we rode in. It smelled good. Sachs was bent over the fire, stirring the contents of a blackened pot, and as I got out of my saddle he straightened up and saw me.

'Hell, Brig, I never known anybody with such timing,' he said. 'The second the grub's ready, there you are.'

I grinned. 'Fill a plate for me,' I told him, 'I'm a hungry man.'

Seth and Joel appeared then, coming out of the black mine tunnel. I watched them come across. They were as dirty as I was, grimed and sweat-streaked.

'Brig, it's good to see you,' Joel said. He grinned at me, his teeth very white against his dirty face. He was unshaven, his hair long and shaggy, his clothes filthy. He looked a different man to the one we had ridden into Hope with and I had a feeling that he was achieving what he'd set out to do, and enjoying it too.

'How's the cattle trade?' Seth asked. He was bent over a wooden barrel, stripped to the waist as he washed the dirt from his body.

I took a mug of coffee, hunkered down by the fire, and relaxed.

'I've got 247 head bunched out on the grass,' I told Seth. 'Good stuff. Not a rib showing in any one of them.'

'What price you pay?' Seth asked then. I told him and he nodded. 'The way they're hungering for beef in Hope you'll be able to name your own price.'

I helped myself to more coffee. 'Way I hear it you may be able to do the same in a while.'

Seth pulled on a fresh shirt. 'Jacob told you?' He joined me by the fire. 'It could be a good job, Brig. I'm like you. I've had my fill of mining. I want something else. Wearing a badge appeals to me. I have a feeling I can handle the job. I'd like to give it a try.'

Joel joined us and Jacob filled our plates. We ate, then sat back and drank coffee. I had some cigars in my shirt that I'd brought from Tarrant and I handed them round.

'We celebrating?' Jacob asked. 'Brig, you ain't sold that herd yet.'

'No,' I told him, 'but I am engaged to be married, so you can wish me luck on that.'

They lit the cigars and then had me tell them everything that had happened to me since I'd left them. My run in with the Reevers was received with interest, but did not raise as much enthusiasm as when I told of my meeting with Judith and what we had planned.

'You see what happens,' Jacob said, 'when you let him off the tether for the first time?'

Seth smiled. 'I'd say that this Judith must be something special if she's affected Brig this way.'

I nodded.

We talked some more and then it was time for me to ride out and take over from Crown and Riley. Jacob said he'd come to keep me company and Joel asked if he could come along too.

We felt the cold night air as we rode away from the fire. It was a clear and sharp night, with a lot of bright stars. I reckoned that there might be a touch of frost by morning.

The herd was quiet. There was plenty of grass around for them. They had come a long way and were tired, and so they were content to just stand and graze.

I sent Crown and Riley back to camp. Sachs had hot food and coffee waiting for them. I told them to get a good night's rest.

'They good men?' Jacob asked.

'Damn good,' I said. 'With cattle and guns.'

I took a slow turn around the herd, Joel tagging along with me while Jacob rode round the other way.

'How's the digging?' I asked.

'Pretty good,' Joel said. 'We hit some hardrock the other day. Had to use powder to break it up but once we were through we found that the vein was still there.'

'What've you got out up to now?'

'I figure we've got about ninety-thousand dollars worth,' he said.

I whistled softly. 'You figure to stick with it?'

Joel tipped his hat back. 'I'll stick,' he said. 'I've got the start I wanted. I won't give up, not until I can go home able to face my father on equal terms.'

'Now that is something I'd like to see.'

Joel grinned. 'Amen to that.'

We reined about to push a few stray beeves back into the main bunch.

'Brig, you're more content doing this than working in the mine, aren't you?'

I nodded. 'And I have a feeling that Jacob and Seth are of the same mind. I guess we just had to let this gold-fever have its head. Well, now we have, and I figure we're ready to move on.'

Joel shook his head. 'If the mine keeps on producing we could all end up rich men.' He glanced at me. 'Doesn't that interest you?'

'It does but I couldn't take being just a man with money. You must know what I mean, Joel. It's the same reason why you're out here digging up a hillside instead of living off your father's money.'

'I guess so. Brig, are you going to settle around here?'

'Maybe,' I said. 'There's some good country up around Tarrant. Fine cattle country. A man could make himself a really fine spread and a good home.'

'I envy you, Brig. I wish I could see my way so clearly.'

'Give yourself time, Joel, and you will.'

'I'd like to meet this Judith of yours.'

I smiled. 'You will,' I said, for I wanted to show her to the whole wide world and let everybody see how lucky I was.

The night passed without incident, the cold leaving a white frost over everything before dawn came. We had a good breakfast, then Crown, Riley and I got the herd off on the last leg of the drive.

It turned out to be a clear, warm day, and we pushed the herd along gently. After what we had just come through, this part of the journey was easy. The way was clear and reasonably flat and we had no trouble.

Close on noon we were reaching the camps and outfits of the people who had chosen to stay out of town. Our passing caused quite a stir and I knew it was the herd that was doing the stirring. Men came running to stare at the beeves and it was almost possible to read the thoughts that were in their minds.

'Hey, mister,' a tall, bearded miner yelled. I reined about as he came up to me. 'That beef for sale?' he asked.

'It will be when I reach Hope,' I told him. 'You can pass the word round.'

The miner grinned. 'Do better than that. I'll let you sell me one of those slab-sided critters here and now.'

'I wanted to wait until I reached Hope,' I said.

'I won't dicker, pilgrim. I'll give you a hundred dollars in gold for one beef.'

I'd hoped for a good return for my investment but this man's offer almost caught me off-guard. Not quite though. I cuffed my hat back, caught Riley's eye.

'Cut out a fat one, Lew,' I called. 'You got yourself a deal, friend,' I said.

The miner grinned at me. 'I've got me beefsteak,' he said, 'and that's worth every cent I paid you.'

'Well you haven't done that yet,' I reminded him.

He pulled his eyes away from the steer that Riley was driving across to us. 'Pilgrim, I haven't had my teeth in red meat for six months. I got a right to be forgetful.' He grinned again. 'Man, am I going to live high on the hog.' A leather pouch appeared out of his grubby shirt. He gave it to me. 'There's a hundred in dust in there,' he said. 'Had it made up at the assay office yesterday. You can check if you want. Tell 'em Clem Yakin sent you. They'll know. They got ten thousand in dust belonging to me in their safe.'

I put the pouch in my saddlebag. 'Your word's enough,' I said.

Yakin nodded. He'd produced a length of rope from somewhere and he was busy looping it round the neck of the steer Riley had brought up. He gave a vague wave of his hand then walked off, leading the surprisingly docile steer like a dog on a lead.

'I ain't seen that done in a coon's

age,' Riley said. He was chuckling softly and I could see the humour in the situation myself. Steers were unpredictable at the best of times, downright vicious sometimes. It wasn't in the wind to go round leading a steer on the end of a piece of rope.

Clem Yakin's purchase brought an instant response from the miners around us and before I knew it I was being badgered on all sides. Pouches of gold and handfuls of banknotes were thrust at me. It seemed that every man in the vicinity wanted to buy his own steer. Yakin had set the price by offering me a hundred dollars and it seemed nobody objected.

It took Crown and Riley and I some time to organise the crowd into a kind of order. It was the only way to make any sense out of it. We sold slightly over thirty head before I had to call a halt. The herd was starting to get upset by all the shouting and jostling. I could see trouble looming on the horizon and I knew I had to do something before the herd decided to cut and run. I'd brought that herd too far, gone through too much to let anything happen now.

'Look, boys,' I called, 'I'll have to call it a day. Any more of this and nobody will be eating beef. That herd's as jumpy as a Mexican bean and all ready to run. I'd like to oblige you all but I can't risk a stampede. Let me drive on into Hope and get this thing done the right way, then there'll be enough beef for you all.'

There was a ripple of grumbles but they all saw my point. Gradually the crowd moved back, letting Crown and Riley and me push the herd together and start it moving again.

I was sweating. That stop had almost got out of hand. I didn't let myself worry too much though. Despite the moment of worry, I had taken in around three thousand dollars and that was nothing to groan about. The bulk of the herd remained untouched.

And Hope lay before us, waiting.

9

I left Crown and Riley with the herd just outside Hope and rode on in alone. All I had to do now was to find a buyer. I didn't figure that would take much doing.

As I rode down the busy street I saw how Hope had changed in the weeks I'd been away. All the tents were gone. Now wooden buildings lined each side of the street. Some were completed, some still under construction. All around were men busy with axes and hammers, saws, paintbrushes. Hope was taking shape fast. I saw nearly a dozen saloons, four eating-places. There was an assay office with a constant stream of men going in and out. I saw a couple of thriving hardware stores, a gunsmith's. And one building that sported the banner: The Hope Sentinel. I realised that events were now to be recorded in the town's own newspaper.

Hope was growing up, becoming more than just a mining camp. It was a good sign, though I knew that there was a long way to go yet. Hope could emerge as a steady community but it would not be without its problems.

I thought about Seth and his desire to take on the job of lawman. It would be no easy task I knew but whatever the odds Seth would prove himself equal to them. Of that I had no doubt.

As I drew level with one of the hardware stores, a man standing on the boardwalk called me by name. I reined in and turned my horse.

The man came to the edge of the boardwalk. He was tall, broad across the shoulders. He wore a dark suit, a white shirt. I judged him to be in his early thirties, though it was a little hard to tell, for he wore a heavy mustache and side-whiskers.

'I know you?' I inquired.

He smiled. His teeth were strong and very white. 'No,' he said, 'but I know your brother Seth. I'm Jonah Sherwood. I'm a member of Hope's town council.'

I got down from my horse and tied him to the hitch-rail. Sherwood offered his hand as I joined him on the boardwalk. His grip was firm.

'This your place?' I asked, indicating the store.

He nodded. 'It is. And I'd like you to come inside for a talk.'

I had a feeling Sherwood was going to talk about more than just the weather.

We went inside. Sherwood led me through the store and into an office at the rear. He closed the door behind him.

'Drink?'

'Thanks. It's been a dry ride.'

Sherwood poured two glasses of whisky. He told me to sit down. He went round to the other side of his desk and settled himself in a leather-backed chair.

'Mr Tyler, I hear you have cattle to sell,' he said.

I nodded. 'Two-hundred-fifteen head,' I told him.

Sherwood leaned back in his chair. 'Mr Tyler, you and I can do a deal.'

'I'll listen to a fair proposition.'

'Then I will offer you seventy-five dollars a head for your entire herd. And I'll pay you in cash.'

I thought about it and tried to work out what it would bring me but I'm a little slow on figures.

Sherwood must have anticipated my thoughts. He gave a friendly smile. 'Don't guess,' he said.

'Figures take me a little time,' I told him.

'Long as the total is right it doesn't matter,' he said. 'Anyhow, two-hundred-fifteen head at seventy-five dollars a head, comes to $16,105. Cash on delivery and I take the herd off your hands.' He glanced at me. 'You want to think on it?'

'I have,' I said. 'You've bought yourself a herd.'

We shook hands and had another

drink. Sherwood brought me pen and paper when I asked for it and I wrote out a bill of sale and signed it. I would have given it to him there and then but he wouldn't take it.

'I trust you,' I said.

'Maybe so,' he said, 'but buying and selling is a thing where trust is a chancy thing. Play it close to the rules, Brig, then you know where you stand. It's the only way to stay sane — and healthy.'

Sherwood had a number of big corrals behind the livery-stable he owned down at the other end of town and we arranged that I would deliver the herd there for him.

'I can have the herd there within the hour,' I said.

We were outside again, watching the busy traffic that filled the dusty street.

'You figure this place is here to stay?' I asked.

'Once we get law and order established,' Sherwood said. 'That's all Hope needs now.'

136

I dusted off my hat. 'Well, I hope you get it.'

'If we can get your brother to wear a badge, then we are well on the way.'

'If one man can do it it's Seth,' I said. 'He'll stand no messing from any man.' I smiled. 'In fact he'll take no interference from those who hire him.'

'I know that. That's one reason I want him. Taming a town like Hope needs a man who can back up everything he does, even if he becomes unpopular with the people who give him the job. I think Seth is that kind of man. And that's what we want right now.'

We talked for a while longer, then I left Sherwood and rode back out to the herd.

Riley had a fire going and coffee on the boil. I had a mug with him and Crown, then we broke camp and set to getting the herd on the move.

Sherwood's corrals were on the far side of Hope, so we circled the herd around the town. The sun was strong now, the way dusty, and we were thankful to see Sherwood's corrals. Sherwood was there, with a couple of men, and they helped us to get the herd into the corrals. It took us a while and by the time we'd finished we were all a lot more dusty and red-eyed than when we'd started.

This time Sherwood took my bill of sale and I took his money. It was a good feeling, knowing that I'd earned that money myself, by my own ability. To some it might not have meant much but to me it meant a lot.

'You think you could bring in any more beef?' Sherwood asked.

'You need more?'

He nodded. 'More people are coming to Hope every day. This herd isn't going to feed many for too long. I'll take all the beef you can bring me, Brig, for cash.'

'I'll see what I can do.'

I rejoined Crown and Riley and we headed into town after we'd stabled our horses. We made the rounds of

138

bath-house and barber shop, then made our way to one of the saloons. I bought us all a beer and we found our way to a table.

'Sherwood wants more beef,' I said as we sat down.

'How much, Brig?' Crown asked.

'As much as we can bring him. Any problems?'

Crown drained his glass. 'No. Only if we go after more beef I figure it might be easier if we had a couple of extra hands along.'

'Fair enough,' I said. 'Joe, you figure you might be able to find a pair around here?'

Crown nodded. 'I reckon so.'

'I'll leave that to you then.'

I ordered another round of beer. We sat and drank, talking casually, letting ourselves relax. I'd decided to lay over in Hope for a day before starting out again. I'd paid Crown and Riley, giving them a good bonus, which I knew they deserved and I realised they'd probably want a little time to enjoy it.

It was late afternoon, though still hot and bright, when we left the saloon. I was getting hungry. We had decided to try one of the eating houses up the street. As we stepped out of the dim saloon into the bright glare of the dusty street I heard a sudden commotion.

Some yards up the street a crowd was gathering. And of a sudden I heard a woman cry out in pain. I simply turned and headed that way. I didn't stop to think. There's something in me that can't ignore the sound of a woman in distress. I know it can mean trouble for myself but I always worry about that after.

I shoved my way through the crowd and found myself confronted by a scene that brought my anger to a head in a heartbeat.

Will Pike was holding a gun on a slim young man who leaned weakly against a hitch-rail, clutching a hand to a bloody arm. It looked too as if the man had undergone a none-too-gentle beating. His face was cut and bruised, his mouth red with blood. He looked to be in pain but I figured that the pain he was feeling was less for himself and more for the girl I'd heard cry out.

She was on her knees in the dust, her slim body twisting about as she tried to avoid the lashing cut of a heavy leather belt that was being wielded at her by a man I recognised the moment I laid eyes on him.

Tall Lyons. Another of Red Karver's killers.

I'd taken all this in during a swift moment. Will Pike still hadn't seen me. I used that fact as I moved. Pike was only a few feet away and I reached him in two steps. My left hand caught his gun barrel, forcing it up into the air, and my right fist took him hard in the side, driving the wind from him. Pike gagged loudly, his knees sagging. I jerked his gun from his hand and tossed it to Lew Riley.

I turned towards Tall Lyons and as his arm swung the belt up for another blow I reached up and caught it, jerking on it hard. Lyons spun round, off balance, and as he faced me I drove my fist into his face. He fell away from me, going to his knees.

'You feel like beating somebody,' I said, 'how about trying me. I'm a little more your size. Trouble is I hit back.'

Lyons' head came up. His eyes were cold. His lips were split where I'd hit him and blood smeared his chin.

'It's the smart-mouthed gold-digger,' he said. 'I knew I'd meet you again, boy, if I waited long enough.'

I unbuckled my gunbelt and handed it to Crown. 'You going to fight or just sit and talk?'

Lyons got to his feet. He was big. Really big. Like it or not, I'd got myself into a close fight and it was going to take more than words to finish it. Of that I was certain.

10

When Tall Lyons moved he moved a lot faster than I'd expected. In fact he moved so fast that I failed to block him completely and his second punch got through. It was a glancing blow that caught the left side of my face, knocking me back. I would have fallen if I hadn't come up against the hitch-rail. I hung there for a moment, trying to clear my head. It felt as if the side of my face had been chopped off. But I had little time to wonder about it, for Lyons was on me almost in the moment my back touched the rail. His big fist slammed into my stomach and I felt my breath burst from my body. I buckled forward and Lyons hit me across the back of the neck. I went face down and if I didn't do something fast I would be down for good and all. Lyons would kill me if he was left to it.

I rolled onto my back. Bright sunlight dazzled my eyes, then it was blocked out as Lyons' body swung into my vision. I saw him lift a boot, ready to stomp my face. I threw up my hands, caught his boot and wrenched hard. Lyons spun out of sight and I let his motion pull me off my back. I hung on to his boot as I came to my feet, then twisted it hard. Lyons had to go with it or let me break his leg. He went with it and hit the ground hard.

I moved in fast, knowing now that he would give me little chance to get any advantage over his size and weight. I stayed to one side until he started to get up, then I moved in and hit him with everything I had. I hit his face and his body, driving him to his feet, forcing him back. The crowd parted, letting us through until we were in the middle of the street. Lyons took it all, took some hard punishment, his face turning raw and bloody as I hammered at it.

I fared little better myself, for though I handed it out to Lyons, he gave back just as well. My body became one bruised ache, my face felt swollen out of all proportion. I could taste blood in my mouth. One eye was almost closed.

I realised that the way things were going we were liable to beat each other to death. Lyons was the sort who would never give up and I never knew when to quit.

But it was Lyons who almost finished it for me. Of a sudden he stopped throwing punches. I had no time to figure out why, for he suddenly threw himself at me and wrapped his great arms around me. I felt my breath being cut off as he squeezed, felt my ribs move. Lyons arched his back, lifting me off the ground. I found myself practically helpless in his grip. He had my arms trapped at my sides. There seemed little I could do. I could feel a surging in my head, an increasing pounding, and I knew that if I didn't do something soon I would pass out.

My legs were free and I figured them to be my only chance. I drew my right leg back and then drove my knee up into Lyons' groin, putting as much force into it that I could. Lyons gasped. His grip slackened for a moment, then he put on the pressure again. I used my knee again, and again, driving at him hard. Lyons hung on for as long as he could, then he let go, a pained sound coming from him.

As my feet hit the ground I staggered, reeling for a moment. My arms felt weak, limp. I worked them, trying to restore the circulation. I kept my eyes on Lyons all the time. He was doubled over, clutching himself, but I knew that as long as he was on his feet he was dangerous.

He moved suddenly, his right hand reaching down to his boot, then coming up and forward. I saw something flash in the sunlight and a coldness hit my stomach as I laid my eyes on the object.

Many men can face a gun and can take it as such but when a knife is produced there comes a moment of something close to panic, a feeling of complete nakedness. Maybe it is the sight of cold, hard steel, the downright deadliness of an exposed blade. What-ever it is I always get that feeling when I see one being used in anger. I've seen what a knife can do to a man and I figure that if I ever had to choose, I'd rather be shot.

I watched Tall Lyons and his knife now and knew that if I made one mistake it would be my last. Lyons would have no second thoughts about using the weapon on me, I knew that. I was going to need to move carefully and when I moved I would have no room for mistakes.

Lyons came at me suddenly, his knife held low, blade turned so that the cutting edge lay uppermost. He moved fast, crouching slightly, his body weav-ing from side to side.

I kept my eyes on that knife, knowing that if I missed nothing else would matter. I was tense, my body tight as a drumskin. I'd chosen to deal myself into this game and now I was having to face the showdown. I was scared but in no way ready to give up. I had too much to live for, too much to look forward to.

As Tall Lyons got close I moved, stepping in close, so that I got inside the range of his knife. It meant that for a moment he had to pause, to change his direction. It was all the time I needed. As I stepped in I turned my body, slamming my right hip into him and catching his knife-wrist with both hands. It meant that my back was to him but I had his knife in sight and partly under control.

We struggled for a moment. Lyons threw his left arm around my neck, trying for a strangle-hold. I shoved my chin down on my chest, keeping him from my throat and then I hung on.

As we wrestled together I was working on Lyons' knife-wrist. I wanted that knife out of the way. Lyons was just as determined to keep it and for a time we were at a stalemate. Then I managed to get my right hand and arm beneath

Lyons' arm. I caught my own left wrist with my right hand, and using a lever action against Lyons' elbow joint, I put on some pressure. Lyons was a strong man. He took a lot before I even got a reaction. But then I heard him gasp, felt his arm slacken on my neck. I gave his arm another few pounds of pressure and this time he gave a grunt of pain. He struggled some but I had him now, and the more he struggled, the worse the effect on his arm. He held out for a little longer. He must have realised that I was in a position to break his arm if I took a mind to. I saw his fingers loosen the knife. It dropped at my feet and I kicked it aside.

I still had Lyons in my grip but I knew that the moment I let him go he would be at me again. There would be no giving up, no quitting.

Letting go of his wrist with my left hand I drove my left elbow back into his stomach. I drove it hard, catching him unprepared. Lyons gave a startled gasp. I spun away from him, turning to face him. He was wide-eyed, his face pale. I'd really caught him where it hurt. I stepped in fast, wanting to finish this thing now. I hit him hard, solid blows that drove the breath from his body before he could recover. Then I hit him across the jaw, a hard blow that laid him out on his back in the dust. He landed hard and lay where he'd fallen.

Of a sudden I felt weak and sick. My face and body hurt. I could taste blood and sweat. I felt like I wanted to lie down next to Lyons.

Then Crown was at my side. 'You alright, Brig?'

I glanced at him, grinning crookedly. 'I think so.'

'You had me worried for a minute or two,' he said.

'How the hell do you think I felt?'

Crown smiled dryly. 'You managed.' He glanced at Lyons. 'You'll have a bad enemy there. He'll have it in for you even more than before now.'

I put on my gunbelt and hat. 'Then he'll have to get in line.'

Will Pike was still standing under the threat of Riley's gun. He watched me as I approached him and I saw hate grow in his eyes. Here was another who had decided I was worth killing. I was getting a little tired of it. All I wanted was to be able to live my life the way I wanted to. I had no intention of bothering anyone as long as they left me alone. But I was beginning to realise that it would be a long time before I was able to do that.

'Give him his gun, Lew,' I said.

'You push your luck, Tyler,' Pike said. His voice was gentle, almost subdued but it was evident that there was anger close behind the outer calm.

'So you keep telling me. And like I said before, I'll be there come the day.'

Pike dropped his gun into his holster. 'With the hired help?' he asked glancing at Crown and Riley.

'That day I'll be on my own,' I told him. 'That's a promise.'

I turned away from him then, going over to the edge of the boardwalk where the girl Lyons had been beating was sitting. The young man was with her and as I approached he glanced up.

'I reckon we look a real beat-up pair,' I said.

He gave a pained smile. 'I guess I asked for it. I took on more'n I could handle.'

'A man can't do any more than try,' I said. 'No reason to be ashamed. My name's Brig Tyler.'

He took my hand. 'Bill Ward. Are you the Brig Tyler who just brought the herd in over the hills?'

'That was me.'

'Some drive,' Ward said.

I'd almost forgotten the girl but I felt her eyes on me now, and I glanced at her. She was young, maybe only eighteen, not much more. Slender and very pretty. She had dark hair and dark eyes, big, bright eyes that were wet with her tears right now. I took off my hat.

'Sorry, Miss,' I said. 'I hope you don't think I was being rude. I surely didn't mean to ignore you.'

'I'm sure you didn't,' she said. Her voice was soft and gentle and she made me think of Judith. 'I want to thank you for what you did, Mr Tyler.'

'It may sound funny, but it was a pleasure,' I told her.

'Excuse me, Mr Tyler,' Bill Ward said. 'This is Madge Novak.'

I nodded. 'A pleasure Miss Novak.'

We talked for a little while. I found out that Madge worked in the store run by her uncle. She'd only been in Hope for a couple of weeks. Apparently she had been alone on the street when Will Pike and Tall Lyons had come out of a saloon. Lyons had been drinking and he'd tried to force himself onto her. Her trouble had been seen by Bill Ward and he had tried to stop Lyons. But Lyons had been too much for him and he'd knocked Ward about for a while before he'd turned his drunken anger on Madge.

Here was a prime example why Hope needed its own lawman. The place was becoming established now, with more families moving in. Women and children needed the kind of protection that only regular law and order could provide. The lawlessness had to be stamped out and stamped out soon.

Madge finally excused herself, saying she was alright now. Bill Ward offered to see her home and she said he could.

'Maybe we'll meet again,' she said to me.

'Under more pleasant conditions I hope,' I told her.

I watched the pair of them go. There was something special in the way that Madge held onto young Bill.

Will Pike had got Tall Lyons onto a horse and the pair were on their way out of town. Lyons was hung over in his saddle, his head down on his chest. He was going to take a long time getting over today's encounter. In fact I didn't really figure he'd get over it at all. Not until one of us was dead.

I figured I'd had enough of Hope for one day and decided to ride out, back up to the mine. I told Crown and Riley.

They fancied staying in Hope for the night. I said I'd meet them back at the mine in a day or so.

I stopped off in a store and bought some personal bits and pieces. I also bought some fresh supplies for the next drive. Outside I loaded everything behind my saddle and mounted up. I rode out slowly. My body was stiffening up some now, my bruises becoming tender. It was going to be a hard ride and I didn't expect to get much sleep when night came.

It was dark when I rode in on the mine. Jacob was on watch but he spotted me a way off.

I tethered my horse, unsaddled and rubbed him down. I gave him feed and water, then made my way over to the campfire and a mug of hot, black coffee. All I wanted right now was coffee, something to eat, then a chance to get into my blankets. It wasn't much. I just wondered if I'd get through this one without being disturbed.

11

Mid-morning of the second day Crown and Riley rode into camp. I was giving my horse a good rubdown. It was good for the horse and it was helping me to work off some of my stiffness. I was still sore from my tangle with Tall Lyons, my body covered in mean bruises, my face still tender, a little swollen. I was getting restless, ready to be on the move again, and I was glad to see my crew riding into camp.

I saw that it had increased in size. Crown had found two more hands and I saw that one of them was Bill Ward. The other was a heavy, chunky man with a very broad chest and powerful arms that seemed on the point of bursting the sleeves of his faded shirt.

Crown came across, wiping the sweatband of his hat. He had a dark bruise under his left eye and a healing cut on his cheek.

'I figured I did enough fighting for this outfit,' I said.

'Was only a friendly tangle, Brig,' he told me, grinning all over his brown face.

'Well, you look as if you've enjoyed yourselves.'

Riley was rolling a smoke. 'You said it, boss.'

'Hello, Bill,' I said as Ward joined us. 'You sure you want to join an outfit like this?'

He smiled. 'If you'll have me,' he said.

'Proud to have you along.' I saw that he was dressed in well-worn trail gear. 'You've been on drives before?'

'Four,' he told me. 'Two up from Texas to Sedalia.'

'Fair enough.'

'Brig, this is Hendrik Carlson.'

The chunky man stepped forward as Crown spoke. He held out a huge hand. His grip was extremely powerful. He had fair hair and pale-blue eyes.

'I see what you do to Tall Lyons,' he said in his broken English. 'Is good. Man who can lick Lyons I will work good for. I am good cowhand. Pretty good cook too.'

'Looks like you're out of a job, Lew,' I said to Riley. 'Lord knows what we'll do with two cooks along with us.'

'I'd say you'll eat pretty good,' Riley remarked.

'All right, Hendrik, you're on the payroll,' I said.

He smiled. 'Is good. And my friends call me Swede. Is easier to say.'

We got ourselves and our gear sorted out and took leave of the mine about an hour later. I wished Seth good luck in the elections for the post of marshal. I didn't envy him the job. If he got it he was going to have his work cut out keeping law and order in Hope.

It was a blustery day. A wind was keening down off the mountain peaks and I could feel a slight touch of frost in it. Summer was fast coming to a close. It was the way of things in this high country. The weather was liable to change suddenly, sharply, and before a man knew it he would be riding through a heavy snowfall. I'd heard this from more than one man who had lived in this country for a number of years. I realised that time was becoming precious and I intended to make this drive in the fastest time possible. As much as I wanted to see Judith I decided to wait until we were on the way back from Tarrant.

The weather stayed pretty clear. The nights became increasingly colder though and on the morning of the second day a light frost covered the ground and whitened the trees and brush.

'Soon there is snow,' Swede Carlson said.

'I hope it holds off until we get the cattle through,' I said.

Swede shrugged. 'Maybe will, maybe won't,' he remarked. 'Anyhow, it take more than snow to stop us.'

I helped myself to coffee. 'If you say so, Swede.'

He grinned. 'Sure thing, boss.'

We reached Tarrant late one afternoon and made camp outside the town. After an early supper we all turned into our blankets. Once we got the herd we were going to be busy so we figured to get as much sleep as we possibly could.

With breakfast over we rode into Tarrant on a morning that was once more white with frost. I left my crew at the saloon while I took a walk over to the bank. I still had all my money on me and I was more than ready to hand it over to George Q. Heath for safe-keeping.

This time there was no nonsense from the skinny clerk, and almost before I knew it I was seated in Heath's office, sampling some more of his brandy.

Heath was extremely interested to hear how I'd got on. When I handed over my money and gold his eyes kind of lit up.

'I'll have this credited to your account this instant,' he said.

'I might want to take some out again later today,' I told him. 'I figure to take another herd through to Hope soon as I can get one together.'

'Do you think you'll manage it before the snows come?' Heath asked.

'It's a chance I'm willing to take.'

Heath nodded. 'I wish you luck.'

I needed speed, not luck, I decided as I left the bank and made my way over to the saloon. I was beginning to get just a little worried about the coming snow. We might easily make it to Hope. Then again we could get caught, herd and all, up in those hills. If that happened we were in for trouble. I didn't let myself be fooled into thinking we would get through all right. Driving a herd through falling snow was no picnic. It was mean work and a sudden freeze could rob a man of most of his herd if it caught him off guard.

Shortly we were out of Tarrant, heading for George Dodd's spread. Dodd was out on his range when we arrived but one of his hands rode out with us to show us where he was.

Dodd was working with his crew mending fences. He left off work as we rode up. I sent my crew over for a mug of coffee as I talked to Dodd.

'I hear you made it,' he said.

'After a few upsets,' I told him.

He cuffed his hat back. 'I figure you stung the Reevers a mite.'

'They asked for it.'

'I guess you are after more beef for the hungry miners of Hope.'

I nodded. 'If you have any. Same price as before.'

'I can see you going far, young feller.' He turned and called to one of his hands. 'I got one-hundred-fifty head I can let you have.'

'I could do with more.'

'Take a ride over and see Ben Choate. He's got some stock he'll let you have.'

Dodd's hand arrived and his boss told him to take half my crew and show them where the cattle were. He wrote out a bill of sale and I wrote out a cheque from a book that Heath had given me. It gave me a strange feeling, being able to write a cheque for a large amount, knowing that I had money to cover it.

I left Crown and Riley to collect the cattle, while Bill Ward and Swede rode over to the Choate ranch.

Choate's headquarters lay in a deep, sprawling basin. A winding creek crossed the land and the place was knee-deep in lush grass. It looked to be a fair spread.

Unlike Dodd, Ben Choate was married and it was his wife who greeted us as we rode up to the house. She was a plump, rosy-cheeked woman of around fifty. She had a basin in one hand and a wooden spoon in the other.

'Well now, you boys look like you rode a long way,' she said. 'How does a cup of coffee and a piece of pie sound?'

I took off my hat. 'Ma'am, it sounds like heaven and we would be right grateful.'

'Then step down and come inside. Only kick off some of that dust first because I cleaned only this morning.'

We got down and tied our horses. Then we rid ourselves of as much dust as we could before we went into the house. Mrs Choate led us through to the big kitchen and made us sit down. She produced an apple pie and a huge wedge of cheese. While we started in on this she brought china mugs and poured us hot, black coffee.

I almost forgot why we were there. The food was good, the coffee even better. I was on my third mug of coffee when a man came into the kitchen. He sat down at the head of the long table. Mrs Choate brought him coffee.

He was a tall man, on the slim side. His hair was silver-grey. He had a strong, lined face, with a wide mouth. His eyes were bright and very blue and he suddenly fixed them on me.

'You're Brig Tyler,' he said. It wasn't a question, it was a statement. 'From what I hear Judith Thorpe has chosen a good man.'

'That's not for me to say,' I told him. I put down my coffee mug. You're Ben Choate,' I said, in the tone he'd used on me.

Choate drained his cup. He gazed at me silently. His face was blank but I was sure I detected a faint twinkle in his eyes.

'Now we know who we are,' he said, 'what can I do for you, Mr Tyler?'

'I'm on the lookout for good beef-cattle, stuff that'll be too old to put on the trail come next spring. I'll take as much as you can let me have. I'll pay twenty dollars a head and I'll pay on delivery.'

Ben Choate squared his hat and got up.

'Ma, give these boys another drink while Mr Tyler and I talk cattle.'

He led me outside and we walked across the dusty yard.

'George Dodd speaks highly of you, boy,' he said suddenly.

'He's treated me fair,' I said, 'and I think I've done the same for him. He's a good man.'

Choate nodded. He glanced at me from under his hatbrim.

'He says you're a mite keen but he figures you'll grow out of it.'

I smiled and saw a faint grin touch Choate's lips.

'What you aimin' to do when you marry Judith Thorpe?'

'I want my own spread,' I told him. 'Up in the country where William Thorpe has his. It's good country up there. A man can put down strong roots and grow.'

'Boy, I'd hate to be anyone who got in your way and tried to stop you.'

'Some already have tried to get in my way,' I said, with some bitterness in my tone. 'Makes a man angry when all he wants to do is to walk his own way and bother no one.'

'I've been in this country for nearly thirty years,' Choate said. 'I've seen it come to life and start to grow. It's got a long way to go yet, though. It'll be a wild country for a long time. We'll get law and order in the end, Brig, but until then every man will have to depend on his own strength if he wants to keep what he's acquired.'

He stopped suddenly, pushing his hat to the back of his head.

'I talk too much,' he said. 'There's a bunch of about three-hundred-fifty head my boys have cleared out of the main herd. I've got them bunched over on the far side of the north pasture. We can ride over and have a look at 'em if you want.'

'I'm ready when you are,' I said.

Two hours later the deal was done and we were driving the herd towards our rendezvous with Crown and Riley.

We pushed the complete herd beyond Tarrant before night forced us to a halt. As darkness fell we bedded down the herd and established our camp. Crown and Riley took the first watch. Bill Ward unsaddled the horses and Swede got a fire going. Shortly he had coffee on the boil, beans and bacon in the pan.

'Boss,' Swede said as he handed me a filled plate.

'What's wrong?'

'We have snow before morning,' he said.

I glanced up at the dark sky. There was a chill in the air, a sharpness in the breeze that came down from the distant peaks.

'You sure?'

Swede nodded. He looked sorrowful, as though any change in the weather was his own fault. 'I am sure, boss. Snow for sure.'

I took the plate of food, helped myself to coffee. As I ate I tried to figure what delay a fall of snow might have on us. It depended on how heavy the fall was. How long it lasted. The way through the hills was raw and unestablished, hard going under normal circumstances. A snowfall wouldn't make it any easier. I figured that there was no profit in worrying too much. The only way to face a problem like this was to wait until it materialised.

I finished my meal and settled down on my blankets. My watch didn't come until just after midnight. It was going to be a long, cold time, and I wanted to get some rest before then.

12

Around about two o'clock in the morning the snow began to fall. It was slight at first but within a half-hour it was coming down thick and fast.

I was well into my watch, along with Bill Ward, and as we circled the herd the snow fell steadily. It layered the ground and the trees and brush, quickly thickening. As I rode I huddled deeper into my coat, wondering just how long this was going to last. It might just be a freak fall, one that would fade out and be over by morning. There was also the chance that it might settle in for a long time. We were pretty high up and the possibility of a heavy, prolonged snow-fall was very strong.

Dawn broke cold and grey. I studied the leaden sky and all the signs said that the snow was here to stay. The sky appeared swollen and heavy, holding the promise of more snow.

The herd was restless and miserable. The cattle didn't like the snow. They knew it meant cold and wet, knew it meant foraging for food. I'd heard it said that cattle were stupid. Maybe so but in some things they knew what was good and what was bad. I hoped the herd wasn't about to get troublesome.

We ate a good breakfast and drank plenty of hot coffee. Every man put on his thickest clothing before we broke camp and mounted up. It was going to be a long day. Little was said. Each man saw to his own task, did it, and then moved on to the next.

The herd took some prodding before it finally moved out. We eventually got it strung out and on the way. We didn't push too hard but let the herd find its own pace. We had a long way to go and I didn't want any trouble.

All through the morning the snow kept falling. It showed no sign of letting up. It fell heavily, colouring the land around us a ghostly white. It broke up the lay of the land, adding to the difficulty of keeping to the trail we had partially broken our first time through.

Towards noon a wind got up and the snow began to drift. It was another hazard to slow us down. We pushed on, keeping on the move. There was little else we could do. The hours drifted by slowly. I realised we were not making a lot of headway. But there was only one thing to do and that was to keep going.

I sent Swede on ahead a way to get a fire going and food ready. By the time we caught up with him he had everything going. We halted the herd and took turns to eat and drink. Swede did us proud. There was scalding coffee, hot bacon, beans spiced with chili, biscuits.

I stood under the drooping branches of a tree, mug of coffee in one hand, a biscuit folded round a thick slice of bacon. Crown was beside me, clearing his way through his second helping of beans and bacon.

'It'll get worse, Joe,' I said.

'You could be right.' He stared out, up at the sky. 'Won't be too bad if the wind don't get too frisky.'

'I figure this'll add maybe a couple of days to the run.'

Crown nodded. 'Three, maybe. We'll make it, Brig. We've got a good crew.'

I knew that. I couldn't have chosen better men. They would stick no matter how bad the going got. I knew I had nothing to fear on that score. But there were other things. The weather itself. The very terrain we were crossing. The herd we were driving. Any one of these things, or a combination of all three, could very well go wrong. No matter which way I looked at it, I could only see a hard trip in front of us. If nothing out of the ordinary took place we were going to have our hands full.

As soon as everyone had eaten we got the herd moving again. It was no easy task. The herd was becoming stubborn. The cattle were feeling the cold and they fancied standing still, bunching together for collective warmth. We had to do some persuading to get them on the trail. Also, the snow was deep enough underfoot to make it hard work for our horses. And that meant we were not able to move around as quickly as we might wish to. All in all it was becoming one hell of a day.

The light began to fail earlier than usual. Coupled with the densely falling snow it made seeing the way ahead more than difficult. I realised that we were not going to get much farther this day.

I located Crown and rode over to him. He had his rope round a steer that had managed to fall into a snow-covered hole. I waited until he had the bawling beef back on its feet and back in the herd.

'Joe, we've got to find somewhere to hole up for the night. It's getting dark fast. We get caught out in the open when the light goes, we're in trouble.'

Crown looped his rope and rehung it on his saddle. He hunched his shoulders against a sudden lash of wind and snow.

'Don't give us much time,' Crown said. 'I'll send Lew on ahead aways. He'll find somewhere for us.'

He reined his horse about and went off in search of Riley. I pushed my horse forward, narrowing my eyes against the sting of hard snowflakes. I noticed it was getting colder.

I caught up with Swede. He was wheeling and turning his horse in and out of the herd, urging the plodding beasts along with a cracking, rawhide whip, and a constant flow of colourful curses.

'Hey, Swede,' I yelled.

He turned his horse my way, coiling the whip as he came.

'You figure on driving this herd to Hope by yourself?' I asked.

He grinned, showing his broad, white teeth. 'We get her there, boss.'

'Lew's scouting out a place for us to use tonight. It's going to be too dark to go any farther soon.'

'Is going to be bad tonight,' Swede said. 'Maybe freeze. Is in the air.'

I nodded. 'I know. I felt it. Let's hope Lew can find us a good place.'

Riley came back about forty minutes later. He pulled his horse in alongside mine.

''Bout half-mile ahead there's a fair-sized canyon with a box at the end big enough to hold the herd. It'll give us some cover from the weather. There's water and grass, some timber. I don't think we'll find anything better.'

'All right, Lew, show us the way. Let's try and get a little more movement out of these beeves else we'll be driving by starlight.'

With Riley guiding us we pushed the herd towards the waiting canyon. It became a race against time. The darkness was catching up with us. And the snow increased in its intensity. It was as if the elements were combining to add to our difficulty.

By the time we reached the canyon we were riding in the thick of a swirling blizzard. The world had merged into one great white blur. A biting wind took the snow and lashed it at us. It numbed the skin, found its way through the very clothes a man wore. It became increasingly difficult to see more than a few yards. We kept contact by shouting to each other. And all the time we were pushing the herd along, trying to keep it together, hoping we were doing it for it was near impossible to keep check on every steer.

Riley fought his shying horse alongside, shouting above the shriek of the wind.

'Straight ahead, Brig,' he told me. 'Herd's just starting to head in.'

'Take them in, Lew. I'll bring up the tail-end. Make sure everybody gets in safe.'

He raised a gloved hand, turning his horse away. He vanished into the snow-mist, swallowed up before my eyes.

I watched the herd drift by me, slapping at them with my coiled rope to keep them moving. More than once I had to turn a stray back into the main bunch before it got lost in the eye-blurring fall of snow.

Eventually the tail-end of the herd drifted past me and I fell in line letting my weary horse find its own way. I could see the high dark walls of the towering cliff into which the canyon cut its way. It rose above me, sheer and stark, for maybe two hundred feet. I peered through the snow and made out the wide, yawning mouth of the canyon. As the last of the cattle went in I gigged my horse forward and a moment later I was beyond the canyon mouth, noticing almost immediately how the force of the wind had dropped. The towering canyon sides cut off the direct sweep of the wind. There was only a cold breeze sifting along the ragged canyon floor. The snow was still falling but not as heavy as it was out in the open. Underfoot it was only a couple of inches deep.

A rider loomed up out of the gloom ahead of me. It was Bill Ward. He grinned at me from out of the folds of his coat collar.

'Lew says not far now. We can push the herd right up to the far end and box it in easy.'

'Glad to hear it,' I said. 'We couldn't have gone much farther out there.'

'Man, I never seen it snow so heavy, so fast,' Ward said. 'You reckon we'll get through, Brig?'

No matter what my thoughts were on the subject there was only one answer I could give him. 'We'll get through, Bill. Don't worry on that score.'

We had little time to concern ourselves about what was to come after we got the herd moving down the canyon. Our full attention was focused on the task of getting the herd corraled in the natural box that formed the far end of the canyon. It took us over an hour, working all the time in falling snow, the light failing fast around us. It got colder with every passing minute.

Once we had the herd in the box we set to on the job of making a barrier across the width of the canyon. We had a couple of axes along with our other gear and we used these to fell a couple of trees. These were trimmed and dragged into position, forming a fair kind of fence. We used rope to lash the trees together. I didn't figure the herd would have too much patience to try and break through. Those beeves were tired and cold. All they would want to do would be to huddle together for warmth. There was grass around for them to feed on. They wouldn't be going far.

Full darkness was almost on us by the time we'd finished. We gathered up our tools and trudged through the snow to where our horses were tethered. Our next job was to find a place where we could hole ourselves up. We needed cover and warmth, a place where we could rest in some sort of comfort.

As we stood together by the horses, a dark figure appeared out of the shadows. It was Lew Riley. He'd been off on one of his forages. He had a nose for scouting things out. He'd found this canyon and if anyone could find us a place to shelter for the night he could.

'Found us a nice place,' he said casually. 'You ain't goin' to believe me but it's a real, nice cabin, all snug-tight and empty. Just waitin' for us.'

13

The cabin lay up a small side-canyon, rising some fifty feet above the main canyon floor. There was a regular trail that led up to it. The trail ended in a wide, level area that was surrounded on three sides by the sheer canyon walls. There were trees and grass and a small stream that tumbled down the sheer cliff into a natural basin.

The cabin was built against one of the sheer walls, this wall forming the rear wall of the building. The cabin faced the trail that approached it. It created a superb defensive position. Anyone coming up the trail would be seen by a person in the cabin long before the cabin came into sight. Whoever had built it knew what he was doing.

Solid logs had been cut and shaped, fitted and locked together with a lot of care and precision. The cabin had been built solidly, meant to last. It had window-holes with hinged shutters. The door was heavy, hung on iron hinges. Somebody had taken a lot of time and trouble over the building of this lonely place.

There was a well-constructed lean-to beside the cabin. We led the horses in and off-saddled. We cleared their coats of clinging snow, fed them with some of the grain we carried for them.

Picking up our saddles and gear we crossed to the cabin and went in. It was dark inside, and musty, the smell that tells you that a place has been empty for a long time. Nobody had lived here for months, maybe even a year.

I heard a match sputter into life. Riley's face was illuminated as he put the match to a lamp. As the lamp flared, then settled, Riley replaced the glass and soft light flooded the cabin, pushing the darkness aside.

Behind me somebody closed the door, shutting out the wind and the snow. I put down my saddle and gear, looked around the cabin's one big room.

There was a handmade table, a couple of chairs. Over against one wall was a low cot, complete with dusty blankets. A fireplace had been built against the back wall, constructed out of natural stone, the chimney going up through the log roof. There were other things, mostly personal items, evidence that at some time, somebody had lived here. There was a long-barrelled, .50 calibre Sharps rifle on wooden pegs over the cot. In the scarred butt were carved the initials J.K.G. There was a three-year old St Louis newspaper lying on the hard-dirt floor under the table. The paper was yellowed, the print fading.

Riley had found a stack of cut wood by the fireplace and he was busy at work getting a fire going. Swede got his cooking tackle out.

'I wonder who he was?' Crown said.

I shrugged out of my wet coat.

'Whoever, he's been long gone from this place.'

Later, as I lay in my blankets, fed, and warmed by the blazing fire, I wondered a little about the man who had built this cabin. Who was he? Was he still alive? If so, where was he? I wondered why anyone should decide to build a cabin in such a lonely place, so far away from anyone. Had he been a man on the run? An outlaw? Or maybe just a man who wanted to be alone, who wanted nothing more than what this place offered? Here a man might find peace of mind, contentment. There was plenty of good, unspoiled land for miles around, the peace of these far-reaching hills. For some men this could be paradise, all they needed to be happy. It gave food for thought.

Though my mind was full of ideas, my body was tired and drained. Now, as I lay relaxed and comfortable, my tiredness caught up with me and I drifted into sleep without knowing it.

I woke as dawn greyed the sky.

185

Slipping out of my blankets I crossed the room and unfastened one of the window shutters. Not too happily I saw that it was still snowing, as heavy, if not heavier, than yesterday. It must have been at least two-feet thick on the ground. I stared out at it for a time and the realisation suddenly hit me that we might easily find ourselves snowed-in, unable to leave this place. If the weather continued this way, we could very definitely find ourselves trapped.

Closing the shutter I made my way across to the fire. Riley had built it up well before we had settled down for the night and it was still burning. I threw on some more logs. Filling the coffee-pot I hung it over the flames, squatting on my heels, staring into the rising blaze.

Had I overstepped myself? Was I going to find myself with a herd of cattle that I couldn't move? Worse, would I lose the herd? It was likely that a freeze would follow the snow. If that happened I was going to be in trouble. I stirred restlessly. I was getting my first taste of the sour end of being in business. It was not to my liking but I knew that if I did lose out I had no one to blame but myself. I had made my choice, taken my own counsel, and had acted accordingly. I could blame only myself.

I didn't sulk for long. I wasn't down yet. Not by a long way. I wasn't down until I had exhausted every possible way out. Until then I was still in business, still on my feet. It did no harm to realise what could go wrong, as long as you still had cards to play.

The coffee bubbled in the pot. I helped myself to a mug. I could hear the others stirring behind me. There was a certain amount of grumbling as they rolled out of their blankets but the moment they smelled the steaming coffee the grumbles ceased. I moved out of the way as they headed towards the pot.

'Gawd,' Riley muttered sourly, 'my

mouth tastes like the inside of a buzzard's belly.'

'Lew, you look like the inside of a buzzard's belly,' Crown told him, his face stoney under his hatbrim.

A laugh filled the gloomy room for a moment, breaking the cramped silence.

'How's the weather, Brig?' Crown asked.

I opened a shutter and let them all see. For a moment there was a hard silence.

'Hell, it looks like we're here for the winter,' Bill Ward said.

'I hope not,' I told him.

Riley poked his head out for a closer look. 'I hope not too,' he remarked. 'Stuck in here with you hombres? Hell, no. You know how long the winters last out here? I'd rather bunk with the horses,' he added dryly.

'Horses are particular,' Crown told him. 'Anyhow, we've been wintered together before.'

'You an' me, yeah. But I don't know nothin' about these other gents.'

'He's worried about your habits,' Crown said solemnly.

Swede, obviously taking the whole episode seriously, pushed out his big chest. 'My habits are good.'

Standing just behind Swede, Bill Ward showed grinning that covered his face. Then unable to hold back any longer he hooted with laughter. Swede looked at him, then back at the poker-faced Riley. He turned his gaze on Crown who failed to hide his amusement. For a moment it seemed as if the big man might let his anger slip. I prepared to step in. But I need not have worried. Swede suddenly relaxed, his craggy face breaking into a wide smile.

The atmosphere was considerably eased after that. We prepared breakfast and sat down to eat. There was a lot of talk and a fair amount of laughter. It was an attempt to keep things running smoothly. Tempers could easily get frayed in a situation like this. Men who spent most of their time out in the open hated to be boxed up for long. They were used to wide spaces, to seeing the earth under their feet and the sky above them. Shut them up in a small room and they soon became a restless, edgy bunch. I'd seen it happen before and I didn't want it to happen here.

After breakfast I sent Swede out to cut some wood for the fire. I put Riley and Ward to tending the horses. Crown and I took a walk down to look over the herd.

The snow was deep in places. We made our way down to the canyon slowly. The sky above was still heavy and full. It looked as if it held enough snow to carry through for a month.

The herd appeared to be pretty well settled in. During the night they had done some considerable moving about, keeping the snow pretty well trampled down. There was ample grass for them and I figured that as long as it didn't freeze, those beeves would manage.

We checked the fence we'd erected. It was untouched.

'Our problem now is to figure when to make a move,' I said.

Crown raised his face to the falling snow. 'Long as it's coming down like this,' he said, 'I reckon we're better off where we are.'

'That's the way I see it. If there was a regular trail I might chance it. Trouble is, we're breaking trail as we go. Too many things we don't know about this terrain yet.'

Crown drew his hat lower across his face. 'We'll rest easy for a while then, Brig.'

'One thing, Joe,' I said. 'Any sign of a freeze, we head out fast.'

We moved back up the canyon, heading back to the cabin. As we crested a ridge in the trail I saw Swede ahead of us. He was just off the trail, swinging his axe at a felled tree. Crown and I moved his way and we helped him to carry the chopped logs back to the cabin.

A little later Riley and Ward rejoined us. We closed the cabin door and prepared ourselves for a day of waiting. Despite how we felt there was nothing else we could do. I didn't relish the thought of sitting here in this cabin for a couple of days. But circumstances said otherwise. Trying to drive that herd in weather like this was plain suicide. The weather was against us and so was the unfamiliar trail. One trip through was not enough time for us to have got a clear picture of the best way. I would have given a lot to have been able to keep driving but I wasn't going to risk the lives of my crew, just to satisfy my impulses.

Riley produced a pack of cards and we got a game of poker started. None of us were real gambling men in the sense that it meant we played for money. We played simply for relaxation, for something to do.

The day passed slowly. We consumed vast amounts of coffee. Just after noon the poker fizzled out. Riley put his coat on, told us he was going to take a turn around the herd. Swede asked if he could go along and Riley nodded.

They hadn't been gone long when Crown got up. He took his rifle and picked up his coat.

'I'll go see if I can find us some fresh meat,' he said.

Silence followed as he closed the door. I crossed over to the fire and helped myself to more coffee.

'Haven't you got anything you want to do?' I asked Bill Ward.

He glanced up from the book he was reading. 'Me? No, I'm fine,' he said. 'I don't take to snow. Much as I like being on the outside. Never did see snow down where I come from. It was all desert.'

'Southwest?' I asked.

Ward nodded. 'Texas. Right on the border.'

'Me and my brothers had an outfit down there before the war. By the time we came back there was nothing left. We could have started again, I suppose, but we had itchy feet.'

'You sorry?'

I smiled. 'No. It was the best thing I ever did.'

Ward came over to the fire. He took some coffee.

'Brig, you do much reading?'

'Some.'

'You figure it's a waste of time? I mean, do you think a man ever learns from it?'

'I think so. I reckon every man has to decide for himself. Some men never look at a book all their lives and they do pretty well. But I think books give you a lot. They open your mind, let you see another line of thinking. Not everything books say is good. A lot is bad, but it is all different. You have to read and then decide if you believe what you've read. One way and another though, I think a man is just that much better off from what he's seen in books.' I paused. 'One thing, it makes you talk a lot.'

Ward smiled. 'Long as it's sense, I don't think it hurts to talk. Man gets too much time alone out in this country. Too much time by himself, too much silence. Gives him time to think and little else. I think some men forget how to talk.'

He held up the book he was holding. 'You ever read any of this feller's work?'

I took the volume. It was William Shakespeare's 'Julius Caesar'. I'd once read his 'Merchant of Venice'. That had been when Jacob and Seth and me had been down in Texas. I'd had a volume of poems by Milton and I had given it to a passing cowboy for the copy of 'Merchant of Venice'. I had spent many happy hours with that book. I'd had it with me during the war but I'd lost it one day during a period of heavy fighting. I recalled that as the day I lost most everything, save for my rifle and my life.

'I once saw a theatrical troupe doing some Shakespeare down in Austin,' Ward said. 'They did bits from maybe four or five plays.' He smiled then. 'You know, Brig, it was a thing I've never forgot. They put up in one of the saloons, set up a stage and all. Come the night the place was packed. Mostly trail hands, all armed to the teeth and drinking fit to bust. Anyhow, the troupe started to perform, and you know, Brig, within five minutes that place was quiet as a graveyard. I don't know just what it was but there was something about that performance that just held a man. Me, I was like most of the others in there. A lot of what was said was way above me. Only it got to me. I figured it was the way the words were put together. You know what I mean?'

'I know what you mean. I envy you that night, Bill. One thing I'd like is to hear Shakespeare spoken like he should be. The way he wrote his plays.'

'Maybe one day you will,' he said.

'If we ever get out of here,' I told him.

He got up and went over to the window and stood looking out for awhile.

I threw some more logs on the fire, then sat back, staring into the flames. I wondered what Judith was doing right

196

now. I realised that this was the first time I had thought of her for some time. Of late I had been too busy to do any thinking at all. I wanted to see her again, as soon as possible. But I realised that I would have to wait until I had the herd safe in Hope. Then, and only then, could I put my mind to other things.

Crown came back after a couple of hours. He'd shot a deer and he set to cutting up the carcass, hanging up the fresh meat to cool.

Riley and Swede returned in time for a fresh brew of coffee. The herd was still all right they told me, and there was no indication of a freeze.

We lazed the afternoon away. I read. Swede settled in a corner and slept. Crown and Riley and Ward started another game of poker, playing for non-existent stakes. By the time darkness fell they were all owing each other vast, impossible amounts.

That night we dined on venison and beans and more of Swede's biscuits. After the meal I took a walk outside. It was still snowing but I had the feeling that it was easing off. I couldn't be sure. I hoped I was right.

I went back inside, fastened the door. I shed my coat, knocked the snow from my boots.

'I think it might be easing off,' I said.

'You certain?' Crown asked.

I shook my head. 'No. I could be mistaken. But if I'm not, I want us to be ready for a quick getaway in the morning.'

We all turned in. If the snow had stopped by morning we were going to have a big day in front of us. We still had a good way to go and there was no way of telling how the weather was going to go. All we could do was to wait our chance, then head out fast and worry later.

I lay in my blankets and it took me a while to get to sleep. My mind was full of jumbled thoughts. But I did sleep and when I opened my eyes light was streaming into the cabin through a gap in one of the shutters. I rolled out of my blankets, went to the door and jerked it open.

It had stopped snowing. A pale, watery sun shone out of a bleak sky. I stood and stared for a moment. I felt anticipation rising in me. Our chance was here. There was no telling how long the snow might hold off. I didn't think about it. I didn't dare because if I did we never would get the herd on the move.

14

We ate breakfast on the run, filled ourselves with hot coffee. Horses were saddled, gear packed. We made sure the cabin was left with a good supply of cut wood, the door fastened. Someone else might come across it one day, someone like us, who needed shelter. Perhaps one day the owner might return.

Down on the canyon floor we dragged aside our fence and rode into the herd. We began the job of getting the herd on the move and it was no easy task, for every beef in that herd had decided that it was pretty well settled where it was. It took a lot of shouting and rope-cracking to break their stubbornness but we finally did it.

Once we had the herd out of the canyon our troubles really began. Ahead of us lay snow-covered terrain unbroken by man or beast. A vast, sprawling carpet of white. It looked all right but there was no knowing what lay beneath that soft whiteness.

I sent Riley on ahead to break trail for us, to try to work out the way which would be safest for us and the herd. I figured that if Riley couldn't do it, nobody could. I soon learned that my judgement was right. Apart from a couple of delays due to floundering cattle we kept on the move throughout the morning and the afternoon. I'd not had to ask if anyone minded going without a break, for Crown had ridden alongside, saying that we might as well keep going until darkness made us halt. I was grateful for that; it made me realise again what a good crew I had.

As the afternoon drew on I told Riley to look out for a place where we could spend the night. Again he did us proud and before the light started to fail we had the herd in a fairly well-protected basin, ringed on three sides by tall trees. A stream cut across the basin, there was ample grass, and the rise of hills around the hollow held off the full force of the wind.

There was a sheltered section of ground on one slope of the basin that was ideal for a camp. We picketed the horses, unsaddled and fed them. Swede got his cookfire going and before long we were tasting our first coffee of the day since breakfast.

I'd noticed a sharpness in the air and I wondered if we were in for a freeze. I mentioned it to Crown.

'Might get a mild frost,' he said. 'I don't think we're in for a bad spell. Not yet.'

'Not freeze tonight,' Swede said. 'Only get cold a little.'

And he was right. The morning was crisp, the air frosty, but it was not anything worth worrying about. It was blowing more than it had the day before. The sky was clear and sharp though.

It stayed that way for the next three days. In that time we made slow but steady progress, eating up the miles that separated us from Hope. We had little trouble, save for the occasional steer that got itself buried in deep snow. It was cold, miserable work most of the time, but we survived, and we didn't lose one steer.

On the morning of the eighth day, close to noon, we passed the edge of the Thorpe spread. I wanted to ride over to see Judith but it would have taken me a couple of hours there and a couple back. There wasn't the time to spare and I knew she would understand.

We made good time that day and camped that night on the edge of a big, deep meadow. The snow was not so heavy here, the weather being a little milder.

'Swede, what do you reckon?' I asked.

'I think maybe we get more snow soon. Not so cold. Maybe one day off, maybe two. But we goin' to get snow.'

'It's going to be close,' I said. 'That last push down to Hope is pretty rough. If we get caught up in another snowstorm we're going to be in trouble.'

'Then we'd better push hard,' Riley said.

We did. The next day we threw that herd on the trail before it was full light. We kept at that herd without pause, driving it on all that day and we were still pushing when darkness overtook us and made us halt. We made camp where we were. The herd just stopped when we did and stood around like it didn't know what to do. There was no fear of any of those steers wandering off. They were dog-tired, just like we were. We ate our food without really tasting it, drank coffee, then pulled our blankets round us and slept until it was time to relieve whoever was on watch.

The next day we repeated the process. We were all tired but nobody let up. Tempers were wearing a little thin by now. We were getting to the stage where we only talked when it was important. Our dispositions were a lot more than sour. We felt sour and I know we looked sour. We were unshaven, unwashed, wearing stale damp clothing. Our faces were red-raw from exposure, eyes aching and red-rimmed. There was no doubt that we must have looked a savage, unkempt crew but I wouldn't have bet on the chances of any man who had told us so.

Again we kept pushing that herd well after dark, only halting when common sense penetrated our tired brains and made us realise we were only asking for trouble. But we had got over the last ridge and we were on the other side of the hills. It was downhill all the way to Hope now. Before us lay the last lap. It was still hard country to cross and not one of us thought things would be any easier even now.

The snow that held off for the past few days caught up with us the next day. It began as a few big flakes about mid-morning. By noon it was coming down thick and steady. It caught us out in the open, on the steep, bare slopes below the timber line, and the wind that came with it tore at us in an icy blast.

I felt a moment of anger. Here we were, so close to Hope, and now we were once more plagued by the snow. My anger faded after a while. There was no future in sitting and cursing the weather. It would have its way, no matter what. All we could do was carry on, keep the herd on the move.

Taking the herd down those rough slopes was the devil's own job. The way was rock-strewn, criss-crossed by gully and ravine. Like the first time across we had our work cut out watching for all these hazards. This time though we had the snow to contend with as well. It hid a lot of the dangers from our eyes.

When something did happen it was not to one of the steers but to one of us. I was riding some way behind Bill Ward when I saw his horse lurch sideways. The animal gave a shrill sound before it, and its rider, vanished in a flurry of snow.

I gigged my horse forward, heading

for the spot where I'd seen Ward vanish. As I rode I yelled to the others, and by the time I reached the spot, Riley was pounding towards me.

I left my saddle in a rush, checking myself as I came to the edge of the deep ravine. It had a lot of brush along the edges and snow had settled on them, giving the impression of solid ground. Ward's horse had stepped onto this false ground, losing its balance and taking its rider with it.

'You see him?' Riley asked.

I pointed. Fifteen, maybe twenty feet below us Bill Ward was on his feet, his face turned up to us. A couple of yards from him his horse was also on its feet, shaken but unhurt. I could see now that the sloping sides of the ravine were thickly covered with brush.

'Bill, you alright?' I called down to him.

'Shook up some but I'm still in one chunk,' he yelled back.

'We'll get some ropes down to you. Get your horse hitched up first then we'll pull you up.'

Crown had joined us by then, leaving Swede to watch over the herd. We snaked out our ropes and tossed them down to Ward. He hitched them to his horse then climbed hand over hand up one of them. We pulled him clear and he flopped down onto the ground.

'You sure you're alright?' I asked.

He nodded. He was pale. There was a nasty scrape down the left side of his face. I kept my eye on him while we hauled his horse up out of the ravine and as the animal came over the top I caught sight of him holding his hand to his right side.

'All right, Bill, let's have a look.'

'It's nothing,' he said.

We got his coat open, then his shirt. It was wet with blood. His side was a mass of scraped skin, the area around already badly bruised. Crown probed with gentle fingers. He sat back, tipping his hat away from his eyes.

'And he wouldn't have said a damn word.'

'His ribs?'

Crown nodded. 'Couple of 'em are busted, I reckon. He's goin' to be one sore cowboy for awhile.'

'I'll manage,' Ward said.

'The hell you will.' I stood up. 'Lew, go fetch Swede. We'll stop here for a while. Get Bill patched up. Day's pretty well gone. We'll make camp over in those rocks.'

We bedded the herd as best we could. Riley and I took the first watch while Crown tended to Bill Ward and Swede got a fire going and food on the go.

The hours dragged by. The snow kept coming. It looked like it was going to settle in again. At least we were close to Hope now. We had made the longest push of the drive in pretty clear weather. I figured I couldn't complain. With a little luck we might reach Hope late the next day or early on the one following.

It seemed an eternity before Crown and Swede came out to take over the watch from Riley and me. We rode back to camp and tended to our horses then made our way over to the fire Swede had left for us. There was coffee on the boil, beans and bacon in the pan. We helped ourselves. I took my plate and mug over to where Bill Ward lay in the shelter of some overhanging rock.

'How you feeling, Bill?'

'Bad about holding you up,' he said.

'Now that is just crazy talk,' I told him. 'You think I mind having to stop because you had an accident?'

'It could make trouble for the herd.'

Riley had heard our conversation. He joined us.

'I think he must have landed on his head, Brig, he's talkin' like an idiot.'

'I keep telling him that.'

'You want anything?' Riley asked.

Ward shook his head. He looked tired. Riley and I left him to rest. We went back to the fire and ate our supper.

'That there boy has grit,' Riley said

softly and he meant every word. He was a tough, rough man, Riley, not given to compliments but he knew when to speak up. 'I'd ride with him any day.'

'You said it, Lew.'

15

In the grey light of dawn we moved out again. It was still snowing and showed no sign of letting up. The wind that had been with us the day before was much stronger now, sweeping down off the high peaks, drawing the snow with it in powdery blasts.

After a fairly good night Bill Ward was able to abide his saddle. He was in some pain but I don't think that wild horses could have kept him out of his saddle. Riley took it on himself to ride close by and to keep an eye on Ward.

The herd had taken a strong dislike to the biting wind and slashing snow. We had our work cut out keeping it together. Twice during the morning the herd stopped altogether and we sweated some until we got it on the move again.

It was colder now. The wind had a raw edge to it that cut through a man like a razor, leaving him numb. I had never been so cold. After a time I began to wonder just what it was like to be warm.

It was close on noon when we reached the bottom of the final slopes. We had reasonably level ground ahead of us now and I figured that if we could keep the herd moving we might reach Hope before dark.

Abruptly the weather worsened. The snow thickened and the wind rose to almost gale force. The buffeting force of it left us breathless. But we pushed on, driving that herd before us. We were too close to quit. I think we would have roped each steer and dragged it to Hope if we'd had to.

Time ceased to exist for us. We seemed to be riding in a perpetual snow, cut off from everything and everybody. We knew only the things that were close to us — the dark bulk of the slow-moving herd, the occasional view of another rider as one of the crew came into sight for a moment. We were alone in the raging, wind-swept storm.

I hardly remember what time of day it was when Riley drew his horse to mine. I turned my head towards him. Beneath the snow that clung to his unshaven face he was smiling. His lips were raw and split and it must have hurt, but he was smiling.

'Brig, we've done it,' he said. 'We're home.'

I followed his pointing finger. For a moment I didn't believe my eyes. But there it was, the buildings emerging out of the swirling snow, smoke rising from the chimneys, lights shining in the windows. We had made it. Hope lay before us. Trail's end.

I think we were all a little dazed at first. It took a while before it came home to us that we had made it, that we were through. Then it did dawn on us and we practically ran the herd over the last stretch. We drove them down to Jonah Sherwood's pens and hustled them in. When the last gate swung shut it was as if a great load had been taken off my shoulders. I stood and looked at that herd and recalled the past days, the effort we had put into getting the herd over those hills. We had pushed hard and we had finally won through.

We mounted up and rode into town. At Sherwood's store I drew rein. I got some money out and gave it to Crown.

'Joe, take the boys and buy them whatever they want. Food, drink. Anything they fancy. I'll see you later, soon as I'm through with Sherwood.'

I tied my horse and went on into the store. It was warm and dry inside. The change hit me like a slap in the face. I made my way to the counter. The place was empty except for a young man behind the counter.

'Mr Sherwood in?' I asked.

He stared at me like I was some walking freak. I realised that maybe I did look a sight.

'I'm not going to eat you, sonny, though I'm powerful hungry. All I want is to see Mr Sherwood. Just tell him Brigham Tyler is here.'

The boy nodded and turned away from me. He went through into the back of the store. While I waited I loosened my coat and pulled off my gloves. After a minute the boy came back. Jonah Sherwood was with him.

'Good Lord, Brig, is it you?' he asked. He looked me up and down. 'Man, you look like you've been through hell.'

He ushered me through to the rear of the store. We walked past his office, into his living-quarters. He had it laid out comfortably. In the living-room a huge fire blazed in the stone hearth.

'Sit down, Brig,' he said. 'Before you fall down.'

I sank into a chair before the fire, letting the heat wash over me. It felt good. I took off my coat and hat, let myself relax. Sherwood appeared at my elbow, a glass of brandy in his hand. I took it and drank. The liquid burned a hot trail down to my stomach.

'Now tell me what you've been up to,' Sherwood said.

'Bringing in a herd,' I said. 'Right now it's all penned up in your corrals. Tallies out to five hundred head. You interested?'

'I've had people in here every day asking when I'll have more fresh beef for them. That first herd went in four days.'

I smiled tiredly. The warmth was getting to me. I wanted to sleep but first I had to settle with Sherwood, then set about getting my crew somewhere to rest up.

'Anywhere in town where I can bed my crew down?' I asked, after Sherwood and I had settled our deal. I folded his check and put it away.

I'd been surprised to hear that a new bank had opened in Hope since I'd been away. Sherwood told me that it was doing a roaring trade and he seemed confident of its continuing success.

'You'll have no trouble cashing that,' he said as he gave me the check.

'I'll take your word for it.'

'That you can do,' he said. 'I'm one of the directors, so I think I can vouch for the bank's safety.'

I smiled. Jonah Sherwood, I realised, was no fool when it came to business. He had a clear head and the ability to see the potential in a place after only a short stay. If he had so much faith in Hope, then it seemed that the town had a good future in front of it.

'Now, about somewhere for you and your crew . . . '

'You don't reckon there'll be any rooms at that hotel they were building when we were here last time?'

Sherwood smiled and I got the feeling he had me anticipated again.

'I figured you might be ready to relax when you got here, so I've had three rooms held over for you.'

'Held over? In Hope? How the hell did you do that?'

I guess I must have sounded a little astounded. I suppose I was. Rooms, any kind of rooms, were pure gold to whoever owned them. Men were willing to pay small fortunes just for the luxury of being able to relax in a clean room, on a soft bed.

'I don't suppose you have some kind of pull with the hotel?' I asked.

'Only a half-ownership,' he said.

'It figures.'

I got into my coat, put my hat on.

'How's the situation on the marshal's job proving out?' I asked.

'We have another meeting in two days. I think I've got Seth in. I hope so. I don't think anyone could match him. Except perhaps you.'

I shook my head. 'Count me out. I'm too quick to lose my temper over some things. Man who takes on a job like the one you have open has to think before he acts. Me, I just walk straight in, settle things my own way. I like the thought of law and order but I don't think I'm the kind of man who could rightly enforce it.'

Right there and then I didn't realise just how soon I was to prove those very words. I was tired and hungry and what

I'd said passed from my mind almost as soon as I'd spoken. But I was shortly to recall my words to Jonah Sherwood, with the odour of gunsmoke in the air and the crash of blazing guns punctuating every one of those words.

16

I had hoped for a good night's sleep and an easy day to follow. I got the first part of my wish, but as I lay in my bed in the light of dawn I was abruptly brought out of my lazy state by a heavy pounding on the door of my room. I heard somebody calling my name and I recognised the voice. Rolling out of bed I grabbed my dirty Levis and dragged them on. I opened the door and Sachs almost fell into my arms.

'Hell, boy, am I glad to see you,' he said.

I led him over to the bed and sat him down. He looked to be in a bad way. His clothing was wet and filthy. His face was grimy, bruised and caked with dried blood, and his hands resembled slabs of raw, bloody meat.

'What happened?' I asked.

'Brig, we got trouble. Bad trouble. I

come to town for help an' heard you'd got back, so I come runnin'.'

I glanced up as Crown appeared in the doorway. He was half-dressed but he had his gun in his hand. Riley was crowding close behind him, Swede as well.

'Tell me what happened,' I said. I was starting to worry. I had a feeling that whatever had happened it concerned my brothers and Joel.

'Late on last night we got raided,' Sachs said. 'It was Karver and his bunch. They just come out of the snow, took us by surprise.' He paused and I had a feeling that the worst was yet to come. 'Brig, boy, I hate to tell you, but they killed Joel. He was facing up to 'em like a real man and they shot him in the back. Some yellow dog come up behind him and cut him down.'

Joel dead. I let the words sink in. A young man with a future ahead of him, that had been Joel. And now he was dead, murdered while he defended what was his against a bunch of killers. He had always worried how he would react if ever the chips were down. It seemed that he had showed his courage but he had not allowed for the treachery of men like Red Karver and his crew.

'Anybody else hurt?' I asked.

'Seth and Jacob are alive but they're in trouble. Karver's bunch set off a powder charge and brought down the hillside over the mouth of the mine tunnel. Seth and Jacob was in there. I took a tumble down a damn gully just after the bang and when I come round Karver's crew had gone. I got over to the mine. Seth and Jacob were all right, bruised up some, but I couldn't move the blockage. There was a lot of big stuff come down with that blast. I told 'em to hang on, then I took my horse and headed to town.'

I reached for my boots, pulled them on.

'Sorry, boys, but we've got some riding to do,' I said.

'We'll be right with you, Brig,' Crown said.

Within a half hour we were riding out of Hope. The snow had stopped falling sometime during the night, so we were able to make pretty good time. The day showed bright and clear, the air was fresh and had an edge to it.

I'd wanted both Sachs and Bill Ward to stay behind but there was no way of making sure they would, short of tying them down. So they rode with us.

It took a while for me to accept that Joel was dead. It was hard. He'd become a good friend. I had liked him a lot and it was a bad way for him to have gone. I would not forget it. And someone would pay. I would see to that. There was an anger in me that wouldn't let me rest until I had settled for Joel.

We rode in on the camp some hours later and I saw straightaway the mass of tumbled rock and earth that covered the entrance to the mine. The blast set off by Karver and his bunch had brought down a considerable section of the hill from above the mine entrance, completely blocking the tunnel. There was a lot of rubble in that pile but it had to be moved. Seth and Jacob were alive at the moment, only they couldn't live too long in their present situation. There were dangers in various forms threatening them now — further rock falls, suffocation if we took too long getting through to them. It didn't warrant too much thinking about.

Once we'd dismounted we rounded up all the tools we could find and then we set on that rock fall. After making sure that Seth and Jacob were all right we wasted no more time on talking. We put everything we had into moving that blockage, using spades and picks without pause, digging until our arms began to ache and our back-muscles throbbed with the pressure we put on them.

Around us the day had grown light and clear. A pale, watery sun shone down on the snowbound land and we paused long enough to shed our bulky coats. And while we dug Bill Ward and Sachs got a fire going, put coffee and food on to heat.

Time passed unnoticed. We knew only that we were taking a long time to move that blockage. Our digging seemed to be having little effect on the earth and rock beneath our feet. But we kept right on digging. We dug and hacked at that blockage until our hands were raw and blistered, our nails split and bleeding. Sweat rolled from our bodies, soaking our clothes, and despite the snow there was enough dust rising from our digging to sting our eyes and coat our throats until they ached.

Yet slowly, so slowly we hardly realised at first, we began to make some headway. Rock by rock, spade by spade, the pile of rubble began to change shape under our attack.

And suddenly I heard a yell. It was Lew Riley, close by where I was digging.

'Hey, I'm through, Brig.'

I fought my way across the loose

surface to where he stood. Riley was on his knees, his pick hacking away at a fair-sized hole that dropped down into what looked like empty blackness. I wasted no time talking. I just added my spade to his pick and we began to widen that hole.

And suddenly I heard a familiar voice. It came floating up out of the blackness and despite the grimness of the situation I had to smile as I heard the words.

'Hell, Brig, what you trying to do? Dig us out or make certain sure we're buried for good?'

Good old Jacob, I thought. It took more than a cave-in to finish off Jacob. It was good to hear his voice.

Before another ten minutes had passed we had got that hole opened up enough so we were able to get a rope down to Seth and Jacob. We pulled Seth out first, then Jacob. He was on his feet as soon as we had him clear but he only took two steps before he fell flat on his face. We picked him up and carried him down to where Seth had been laid on a blanket by the fire. They had both been pretty badly banged about. When we got them stripped-off it was plain to see that they were going to be might sore in a while. Great bruises and grazes covered them from head to foot. We cleaned them up as best we could, put them into clean clothes, then fed them.

It was a little after that when I found myself alone, some way off from the others. I was standing beside a laid-out shape under a blanket and I was trying to remember the sound of Joel Welcome's voice, the way he smiled, or the way he moved his hands as he spoke. The hardest thing in my mind was the fact that it was already becoming difficult to recall these things. But I didn't forget what he had meant to me, the relationship that had developed between us. It was something I was not likely to forget.

I was angry too. Angry at the way life and property was so casually destroyed by men like Red Karver, Will Pike, and

Tall Lyons. It was because of men like these that Seth and Jacob lay hurt, having come close to death. And it was because of these men that my friend Joel now lay dead, his young life snuffed out just as he was getting his first foothold.

The more I thought about it the greater became my anger. I'm not normally a vengeful man but vengeance was strong in my thoughts right at that moment. The utter ruthlessness of Karver's action kept pushing to the front of my thoughts and a taunting voice seemed to be telling me that this was the way Karver had been operating for a long time and getting away with it. He got away with it because nobody ever stood up to him. Too many people were getting hurt and nobody wanted to get involved. Karver knew this and he played on their fear. It kept him on top. His confidence fed itself on the fear of others.

But Karver had made a mistake this time. He didn't know it but he would do shortly. I went to my horse and got him ready to ride. I knew what I had to do, what I was going to do, and I just hoped that nobody got in my way.

Crown wandered across as I stood by my horse, thumbing fresh loads into my handgun. He watched me for a moment.

'Need anyone to ride with you?' he asked finally.

I glanced at him. 'You figure I'm going somewhere?' I asked.

'I figure.'

'Thanks, Joe, but this one is mine. No room for anyone else.'

He nodded. 'Ride careful, Brig, that Karver bunch is all bad and mean as hell.'

I mounted up and took my horse out of camp without looking round. I knew I could be riding into more trouble than I could rightly handle but it did nothing to make me think twice about going. What I had to do was something from which there was no turning back. I was scared some, no use pretending I wasn't, yet even that made no difference. I only had to think of Seth and Jacob and of Joel and all thought of quitting left my head. I was a little mixed up inside but on the surface I tried to appear calm. In a while I was going to need all my wits about me. I would need to be calm and steady and clear-headed.

It was late in the afternoon when I rode into Hope. The place was as busy as ever. It seemed almost wrong that life was still going on here, as though nothing had happened. Then I realised that I was thinking too much about things that were important to me. The killing of Joel Welcome would be little more than one more chunk of news to the people of Hope. To them he would be a name without a face, just another victim of this wild and violent land.

I reined in before one of Hope's many saloons. This was the place where Karver hung out. He used the place almost like headquarters while he was in Hope. I wondered if he was in there right now. Knowing him like I did I reasoned that it was easily possible. Karver would have no qualms about returning openly to Hope, even though he had just committed murder.

As I sat there the swing doors parted and a man came out. He had a bottle in one hand and a couple more tucked under his arm. I called to him and he came to the edge of the boardwalk.

'I'm looking for somebody,' I said. 'Name of Red Karver. You happen to see him in there?'

The man took a hefty swig from his bottle. He screwed up his face as if he didn't like the taste of what he was drinking.

'He's in there,' he said. 'Him and Tall Lyons, an' they're drinkin' like it was going out of fashion.'

'Any more of Karver's boys there? Will Pike maybe?'

'Only the two of 'em. Karver an' Lyons.' He eyed me boldly. 'You a friend of 'em?'

'Kind of,' I told him as I got down off

my horse and tied the reins to the hitch-rail.

My informant watched me as I stepped up onto the boardwalk. He seemed to be debating something with himself. When I took out my gun and checked it he suddenly came to a dead stop in his debating. He turned on his heel and moved off up the walk.

I stood before the swing doors for a moment. Right there and then I had no idea what might happen once I went through those doors. A lot hung on what took place in that saloon. My future with Judith, my future with my brothers and the men I knew. All of these things could be lost to me in the next few minutes. I knew that but I also knew that if I didn't go inside, if I walked away, I would never be able to face myself again.

I found myself thinking of Joel again. Joel, so young and full of ideas and ambition, driven by his father to prove himself able to stand on his own. He had done just that but he'd had no chance to enjoy that victory, and he never would. I remembered these things and it was that remembrance that propelled me across the boardwalk and through the doors, taking me into the saloon's noisy, crowded interior.

17

As I eased my way through the crowd I saw Red Karver at the bar. His loud voice could easily be heard, even though there was some considerable noise. Karver was not alone, as I had been told. Tall Lyons stood next to him and as I neared them Lyons spotted me and nudged Karver. Turning from the bar Karver faced me, a confident look on his broad, ugly face.

Behind me the crowd suddenly quietened and I heard chairs scrape and boots scuff the wood floor. An empty space appeared around me as the crowd drew back. It was as if they knew why I was here, what I had intended.

'You lookin' for me, Tyler?' Karver asked. He had moved away from the bar a little, so as to have an area of free movement.

'I've come to even things for Joel

Welcome,' I told him and I could tell by his eyes that he knew what I'd come for.

He tried to bluff me out by laughing. 'Now what do you mean by that? Who is this Joel Welcome you're talkin' about?'

'The boy you cut down last night,' I said.

'What's that you're callin' me?' he asked and his tone was one of outraged defiance.

'A murdering backshooter,' I said. 'You couldn't scare my brothers or Joel off our claim, so you tried to drive them out. You almost killed Seth and Jacob with that cave-in but they're alive. But you did kill Joel. Shot him in the back without giving him a chance.'

Karver was red-faced now. His right hand was flexing impatiently over his gunbutt. 'I hear you right? Accusing me of murder?'

I didn't answer this time but let the heavy silence drag on. Karver's eyes flicked around the crowded saloon. This was the first time that anyone had ever made an open challenge to him. Maybe he was a little scared, maybe just a slight confused. I wasn't sure which but I knew that something was due to happen.

Tall Lyons had begun to edge away from Karver. He was trying to distract me, I knew, trying to make it more difficult for me to watch them both. I knew that if I let it happen I would find myself in a crossfire.

'Lyons,' I said, without taking my eyes off Karver, 'just stand easy. You move again and I'll drop you first.'

My tone must have convinced him for he stopped moving and leaned casually back against the bar, his hands in plain sight.

Karver, somewhat more himself again, said, 'What you aimin' to do with me, boy?'

'Like I said, I've come to settle with you for Joel Welcome. I know, and every man in this town knows, you're a thieving murderer. You need putting

237

down like a mad dog but I'm ready to give you a chance. That's if you've got the guts to face a man who can shoot back.'

A smile played round the edges of Karver's mouth, then vanished. He spat suddenly. 'You figure you can take me?'

'I didn't come to talk,' I told him.

Karver took a short step forward, and I tensed, knowing that something was about to happen.

On Karver's right Tall Lyons' hand eased towards his gunbutt. His hand was partly hidden by the way he stood but the movement was enough to catch my eye. I let my gaze flick towards Lyons, only for an instant, and as I did I realised I was being drawn into a trap.

The second I took my eyes off Karver he went for his gun, and by the time I'd figured what was going on, he had it halfway drawn. If he'd been any faster I would not have walked away from that fight.

My own hand was sliding my Colt free as Karver's gun rose and even in that moment of danger I heard the hammer go back. Then I threw myself forward, below the level of Karver's gun. I hit the floor hard and as I did I pushed my drawn Colt forward, tilting the barrel up. The hammer was back and I pulled the trigger, putting a bullet into Karver, saw him step back against the bar. His gun went off, the bullet going into the ceiling. He wasn't about to give up though, for he made to pull his gun on me again, so I fired once more. The bullet caught him high in the chest and he spun sideways, going to his knees.

As I triggered my second shot I arched my body around, my eyes seeking Tall Lyons. He had his gun out and he pulled the trigger as I turned to face him. I felt his bullet burn my left shoulder but then I had my Colt on him, and I triggered two fast shots into him. My bullets took him in the chest, angling upwards and bursting out of his back. Lyons gave a ragged grunt and skidded along the edge of the bar for a way. Then his legs gave and he fell onto his face.

I rolled and came to my feet, turning, and as I did Red Karver's gun roared. I felt the bullet hit my left side. The impact knocked me back a few steps. Then I swung my Colt and tripped the hammer back, bringing it to bear on Karver. He was on his knees, his left hand pressed over a spreading patch of blood on his chest. He was weak, losing a lot of blood, but he was still capable of handling a gun. He was dogging back the hammer again, and for a moment our eyes met, hate blazing in his as he faced me. I put my last two shots into him and he toppled over onto his back, his gun spilling from his fingers at half-cock.

I stood where I was for a moment. The stench of gunsmoke was heavy in the air. I felt a little dizzy. The wound in my side was starting to pain me some. Blood was covering my shirt and Levis. I put my empty gun away and turned slowly away, went out of the saloon, onto the street, ignoring the stares and sudden sound of raised voices. I paused on the boardwalk, breathing in the clean air, trying to calm my jangled nerves. It had come close in there. Too close. I had bucked the odds, risking my life, but it had been something I had to do. I had no regrets about killing Karver and Lyons. They had been of a kind that was all too evident in this violent country. As long as there were men who would work and sweat to develop the land's riches, there would always be others who would come and take the result of those labours by force and violence. And until the law was established every man was going to have to do his own peacekeeping. I figured I had done my share this day.

I got onto my horse and turned him up the street. I rode out of Hope, heading back to the mine. I had a long three hour ride ahead of me and I wondered if I could stay in the saddle that long. It was turning cold again, my wound hurt, and I felt sicker by the minute, but I knew I had to stay in the saddle.

I never did remember the whole of that ride. A lot of the time I was close to passing out, but somehow I rode the entire way without falling off. I recall hearing Sachs shouting as my horse took me into camp. I forced open my eyes and saw him running towards me, with Joe Crown close behind. Then I just let go. Darkness swept over, the ground rushed up to meet me, and I blacked out.

18

I spent the next three days on my back, recovering from the wounds I'd received during my clash with Red Karver and Tall Lyons. I'd lost a fair deal of blood during my ride back to camp and although I wanted to be up and about I was too weak to be of much use to anyone.

Seth and Jacob fared some better than me. After a good day of rest they were able to start moving around again. They were stiff and sore, but apart from that there was little wrong with them.

On the second day Crown and Riley took a ride into Hope. When they came back late that evening they brought us up to date with the news from town. High on the list was the run-in I'd had with Karver and Lyons. It seemed that I'd started something. Every man who'd ever run with Karver had been told to get out of town. The order also extended to cover any man who figured he was in Hope for what he could get, by foul means. It meant that a lot of toughs and potential gunhands received the order to quit camp and move on. A vigilante group had formed to help them on their way.

'One thing, Brig,' Crown said. 'I heard that Will Pike's been bragging.'

'Now that sounds like trouble,' I said.

'It's not a friendly greeting. Seems he's joined up with the Reever boys now. Only he's been saying he'll kill you next time he sees you. One day he's going to meet up with you and finish what you've started.'

'He'll have a long wait,' I said. 'I'm not hunting trouble. If it comes I'll face it but I won't go looking for it.'

Jacob leaned forward to refill his coffee cup. 'Brother,' he said, 'I don't think that will stop it happening.'

And though I was reluctant to agree with him, I had to admit that Jacob was right. But right there and then I don't think any of us knew just how soon the matter would be resolved — or the way it would happen.

The second day since I'd been allowed to get up was clear and bright. A lot of the snow had cleared and what was left was thawing slowly. The air was fresh and good to breathe. I stood on the edge of camp, gazing out over the spread of the country that lay below our high place. A lot of greenery showed through the blanket of snow. The sky above was washed blue, with streaks of cloud. To the eye it was good land, spreading as far as the eye could see and then some. But it gave a man reason to pause when he thought what had to be sacrificed in order to tame the land. I was thinking of Joel. I wasn't given to brooding but I was still feeling a great loss.

Karver and Lyons were dead but that didn't bring Joel back. He was dead too and it was hard to realise. We had buried him just beyond camp, close to a stand of shady trees where he'd used to go and read. It was a quiet, peaceful spot and we had figured that it was a place he would have chosen himself. Sachs had cut a wooden marker and he'd carved Joel's name on it like it was his own son he was burying. I'd taken it on myself to write to Joel's father. It had taken me some time but I'd had a lot to say. I'd hoped that I had explained the way Joel had felt, why he'd come West, what he'd wanted to do. I'm not too good with words but I think I managed to say it all. If I'd been Joel's father and if I had got such a letter, I would have been proud to say that my son had lived like a man, had made his way, and that though he had died, he had made his mark and had more than proved himself.

Yet I could not hide the fact that I would rather have had Joel himself standing beside me. All the words in the world could do little more than ease the sorrow. Only time could completely heal the hurt.

I heard Sachs calling me. It was close

on noon and he had been getting a meal together. It seemed that all we had been doing for the past few days was eating and lazing around. I realised that it was time we all began to organise ourselves, to get our plans set out.

As I headed back into camp I happened to glance up at the tall hills beyond and saw a lone rider coming down out of the trees. I stopped and watched, for there was something familiar about the horse and the man riding it. It was the horse that I recognised first and with that recognition came shock. The horse was the one that William Thorpe rode and a moment later I saw that it was Thorpe who was riding it.

My first thought was for Judith. Had something happened to her? Was she hurt? Or worse? I brushed such imaginings aside. But I was sufficiently worried so that I crossed over to the horses, mounted up, and rode out to meet William Thorpe.

I reined in before him and saw

straight off that something was wrong. Thorpe was dirty and unshaven, he looked tired too. There was a recent gash on the left side of his face, crusted with dried blood.

'Thank God I've found you, Brig,' he said. He gripped his saddlehorn. For a moment it seemed he might fall but he pushed himself upright.

'What's happened?'

'Will Pike and the Reevers raided the ranch. I tried to stand them off but there were too many. I had to quit, Brig, before Judith got hurt.'

I had a feeling there was more to come.

'How is she?' I asked.

'They took her, Brig. There was nothing I could do. Will Pike said she would come to no harm. They took her for a hostage, so they'd be left alone. They run off the herd as well, not that it matters. But Judith does, Brig, and we've got to get her back.'

'We will,' I said.

We rode on into camp. My mind was working furiously. Will Pike had known exactly what he was doing when he'd taken Judith. Nobody else might have known but I did. He knew that I'd go after him the moment I heard what he'd done. And he was right. He was setting it up so that we would come to a showdown. If that was what he wanted, then he would get it. There was nothing that could prevent me from going after him now, short of being dead. Will Pike was a marked man now. Maybe he didn't know it but he had set me on a trail that would only end when one of us was dead, and I had no intention of it being me.

While William Thorpe sat down with food and drink I laid out the situation for the others. I didn't ask anyone to come along. I didn't have to. There wasn't a man there who would even have hesitated if I asked. I considered myself a lucky man to know them. Two of them were my brothers, I know, but it still gave me a good feeling.

We all ate first, then got our gear ready. Sachs piled foodstuffs into a couple of flour sacks. I broke into the ammunition supply I'd bought in Tarrant, passing it around. The way things were going it looked like we were going to need it.

William Thorpe took the lead as we rode out, up into the hills. I was glad that the snow was thawing. We would be able to make better time. Pike and the Reevers had a good start but they were hampered by the herd they were pushing. We had only ourselves to push.

We rode the rest of that day and all through the night. William Thorpe knew the hills well. He'd made sure of the way Pike was heading before he'd come after us and now he led us by the most direct route to intercept the trail of the outlaw bunch.

Dawn found us high up. We were riding through heavy-wooded country now, thick with brush and grass. If we'd had time to look we would have seen that it was good country, green and pleasant. But we had no such thoughts on our minds.

Ahead of us the hills merged into rugged mountain peaks. They swept up into the empty sky, dark and cold-looking, the tips of the peaks white with snow. Pike and company would be heading that way, hoping to leave the territory by crossing the mountains. If they reached those mountains before we caught up with them our task would be one hell of a sight harder. A whole regiment could hide itself in those towering expanses of rock.

At noon we stopped long enough to rest and water the horses. Swede got a fire going, put coffee on. We ate bacon and beans, biscuits, and drank coffee. A short rest and then we were in the saddle again.

Once more we rode all night, helped by a full moon as we had been the previous night. Thorpe led us through a land turned to velvet-soft shadow and silver light. With the darkness came the cold and we put on coats and gloves to hold back the chill.

The new day found us in a land of

canyons and deep ravines thick with brush and trees. High green slopes rose all around us. It was perfect ambush country. It made a man feel exposed and naked just thinking about it.

About mid-morning Riley, who had gone on ahead, rejoined us. I could tell by his expression that he had found something.

'Up ahead,' he said, 'is where they camped last night. I figure they're no more than two hours in front of us.'

I let Riley take the lead now. We pushed on fast, covering the gap that separated us from Pike and the Reevers in good time.

And suddenly Riley threw up his arm, reining in his horse. I rode to join him. He pointed and I followed the direction of his finger. We were on the crest of a tree-filled slope that curved down to a sun-dappled narrow canyon. And down there, strung out in a long line was William Thorpe's herd, with riders hazing it along.

I scanned the horses and riders.

Where was Judith? I wanted to see her, to know she was still all right. And then Riley touched my arm and pointed again. I looked. It was Judith. She was wearing the dress I'd brought her from Tarrant. Will Pike was riding the horse next to her. I felt my anger starting to rise. I clamped down hard. This was no time to start getting reckless.

The rest of our crew had reached us now and for a moment we all sat and watched the progress of the outlaw bunch down on the canyon floor.

I turned to William Thorpe. 'How many were there?'

'Thirteen altogether,' he said.

'Fair odds,' Riley said.

'There's only nine of us,' I said.

Crown glanced up from checking his handgun. 'Lew always likes it a little thick. Gives him a chance to be selective.'

Before anyone could say anymore a rifle shot broke the leafy calm and a rider broke from the trees midway down the slope, heading back to where the herd threaded its lazy way. We had been spotted. I forgot all my notions of a surprise attack. All we could do now was to wade on in and have it out with Pike and his crew.

'Try and make every shot count,' I yelled as we took our horses down the long slope.

As I rode I tried to keep my eye on Pike and Judith but I lost them in the sudden confusion. It seemed like every gun in creation had opened up. Bullets hummed through the air like angry wasps. They clipped the leaves and chewed chunks of bark from the trees.

As I felt my horse hit the canyon floor I swung from the saddle. My handgun was empty and I grabbed my rifle and jacked the lever. There were a number of empty saddles and more than one man down on the floor. I had no time to notice who they were.

A big man on a black horse was suddenly before me. He had a gun in one hand and he fired as he got it lined on me. I felt the bullet clip my sleeve.

Then I upped my rifle and drove three quick shots at him. Dust flew from his shirt as my bullets caught him in the chest. He fell backwards out of the saddle and hit the ground on his face.

I realised that I was more or less out in the open, too much exposed for my liking. I headed for a large, scarred rock but as I neared it I was suddenly confronted by a dark-haired man with a bleeding gash down one cheek and gun in one hand. He was a big man and I recalled seeing him with the Reevers when we'd had the run-in during the first drive.

For a moment we were motionless. Then we both moved. He swung his gun up at me, dogging the hammer back. I leaned in on him and swung my rifle at him. The butt cracked down across his arm. I heard bone crack. His gun went off, the bullet plowing into the ground at our feet. I swung my rifle again, driving the butt into his face. He gave a gurgling yell and went over backwards. His head slammed onto hard rock as he hit the ground and his body arched in pain. He flopped over onto his stomach. The back of his skull had cracked and had split open like a crushed eggshell. I turned away, feeling sick.

A bullet howled off the rock close by. Sharp chips of stone stung my cheek. I eased myself behind the rock and returned the fire, loosing off three or four shots. I saw a man throw his arms wide, stumble and fall.

The heavy gunfire began to slack off. I saw a man emerge from cover, throwing his gun out before him. Then another one appeared. I came out from my rock and stepped out into the open. Crown stepped into view. He had his gun in his left hand. His right arm hung at his side, his shirt sleeve bloody.

Bill Ward rode out of the trees nearby. He had his rifle trained on a thin, dark-faced man who was nursing a bloody leg.

'Brig, Pike and the Reever boys took off with Miss Thorpe. I saw them riding over yonder ridge.'

I looked round for my horse. Locating it I went over and gathered the reins. As I led it back to where Crown and the others were standing I saw Swede coming across the canyon floor. He was carrying someone in his arms and a hard knot of coldness hit me as I saw who it was. Jacob was close behind him, his face tight.

Swede knelt down and gently laid William Thorpe on the grass. I didn't have to speak the words that were in my thoughts. I only had to look at the patch of blood on Thorp's shirt, the dark hole in the centre, right over the heart.

'He didn't know it had happened, Brig,' Jacob said. 'He'd just put down a man who had a bead on me. Jack Reever took him with a rifle. If I hadn't run out of shells I might of stopped it.'

First Joel Welcome, now William Thorpe. Two good friends dead, killed in a few days. I wondered how I would break the news to Judith.

But first I had to get her back, away from Will Pike and the Reevers. I had to get her away before they did anything to her. Pike's plan had not gone as smoothly as he had anticipated. He would be touchy now, ready to hit out at anything and anyone. Right now Judith was the closest in line.

I reloaded my guns, made sure I had spare ammunition in my belt.

'Brig, you figure on going alone?'

I glanced at Seth, for it was his question.

'I'm going to fetch Judith back, Seth, and I don't want anyone in my way.'

'It's three to one, Brig,' Seth said. 'Don't you think the chances would even out if Jacob and me came along?'

'You know how I feel about you two. But this is my fight, Seth. Will Pike wants a settling and so do I. Look, Seth, he's taken the girl I'm going to marry. He's going to have to answer for that. And to me only.'

He stared at me hard for a moment. Then he nodded slowly. A faint smile touched his mouth.

'All right, little brother,' he said. 'But you take care. We want you back alive. You and Judith.'

I mounted up and turned my horse towards the ridge where Bill Ward had seen Pike and the Reevers and Judith go.

Behind me the remaining Reever men were being disarmed and herded together. They would each be given a horse and told to ride out of the territory. I figured that they would do just that. Rough and tough they might be but they had sense enough to know when to quit.

As I headed for the ridge I passed the scattered herd. A touch of regret hit me as I saw those cattle. William Thorpe had had plans for them. He'd wanted to build a herd that would be known far and wide. He had died for that idea. I hoped that I wouldn't let him down on the dreams I'd laid out before him, the life I had promised his daughter. I thought of Judith. There was no question — I had to reach her, take her from Will Pike before he decided she was of no further use to him. Once he had reached that decision her life would matter very little to him.

19

Beyond the ridge the tracks were easy to follow. Four horses and they were moving fast, not bothering to cover their backtrail. Plainly they expected to be followed, maybe they were hoping to be followed. Will Pike knew enough about me to realise that I would follow him. He had Judith and he knew I'd never quit until I had her back. He was using her as a lure, sure that I would come after her, and him. He was right. Follow I would and he would get his showdown.

I pushed my horse as hard as I dared. The way was difficult, heavy brush and tumbled formations of rock making fast riding dangerous. But I had only one thought in mind. Judith. I had to get to her before she was harmed. I had no illusions about the kind of men who held her. They were violent, wild men who held little regard for anything or anyone. In general the men of the West, though rough and ready, were noted for their respect of womenfolk. A man could get away with a lot but let him mistreat a woman and he was asking for trouble. Pike and the Reevers had no worries on that score. It made little difference to them what they did. In their regard for human life they were the lowest of the low. And it was that fact that bothered me most. Let them decide that Judith was in their way and they would kill her without thought.

This thought was what drove me on, urging my horse through the brush at breakneck speed. I had to reach Pike and company before darkness came. Once night fell they would have a better chance of getting out of sight. They could hole up or set an ambush at their leisure.

I figured it to be mid-afternoon when I spotted them for the first time. They were above me, walking their horses up a long, rocky slope. They were about a half-mile in front of me. Above them was an area of treeless hillside, a jumble of bleached, tumbled rock, stretching in both directions as far as the eye could see. Once they got in there it was going to be difficult getting them out.

By the time I had negotiated the long slope and had rested my horse for awhile, more than an hour had gone by. I had neither sight nor sound of Pike or the Reevers. They were somewhere in the rocks that stretched out before me. They could be deep in the jumbled mass by now, I realised. Then again one of them might be hidden behind the nearest boulder. A rifle could have been trained on me right there and then.

I got down out of my saddle and took my canteen. The water was warm, but at least it quenched my thirst. It was warm up here. There was very little snow on this bare face of the hills. I noticed how silent it was up here. There was nothing but the sky and the hard, dry earth. There wasn't even the sound of a bird, the buzz of an insect. I didn't mind a peaceful sort of silence but the utter deadness of this place was liable to upset my nerves.

I put my canteen back on my saddle and took my rifle, levering a round into the breech. I figured to do a little looking round before I went any farther.

And then the whipcrack report of a rifle shattered the silence. I felt the tug of the bullet as it clipped my left shirt-sleeve. I threw myself face down, my own rifle thrust forward.

The hidden rifleman fired again, his second bullet kicking up dirt only inches from my face. I rolled off to the right and as I came to rest I fired at the place where I'd spotted a puff of smoke. I must have come close for I heard a sharp yell, then saw a figure push upright from a low rock. Whoever it was he didn't figure to stand and fight, for he turned and vanished into the maze of rocks at his back. I shoved to my feet and took off after him, not worrying too much about cover. I was close to becoming a slight angry, and when I get in that frame of mind I tend to let caution slip. Just of late I'd been shot at and generally knocked about to the point where I'd had enough. I'd lost two good friends at the hands of some of the territory's worst scum and I was more than ready to start kicking back. I'd never in my life deliberately gone looking for trouble but here and now I was itching to start some.

I hit those rocks at a dead run, my eyes searching ahead of me for the ambusher. For a couple of minutes it seemed as if I'd lost him but then he showed himself some way ahead. He was dodging in and out of the rocks like a scared rabbit. I halted long enough to throw a shot his way. My bullet clouted rock close to him and he stopped dead for a second, turning to look my way.

I didn't need a second look to recognise who he was. Thin, with a dark beard. Wearing a faded rose-coloured shirt and striped pants.

Jack Reever.

He put up his rifle and fired. The bullet made a high whining sound as it skimmed off rock just inches away from my left foot.

My reaction was automatic. Almost without thought I upped my rifle and took quick aim, fired, levered, and fired again. I saw Jack throw up his arms and stagger back, fall out of sight.

I made my way over to where I'd seen him drop. As I got close I eased off. I didn't know how bad he was hit. I didn't know if he was hit. More than one man had been suckered into a trap like that. I moved slowly, making as little sound as I could.

I reached the large rock that hid Jack Reever from my sight. I put my rifle down and took out my handgun, easing the hammer back. Gently I began to move around the rock.

And then Jack's rifle fired, almost in my face. I threw myself to one side, twisting my body away from the bullets that came at me. I went to my knees, slamming the side of my head against hard rock, but I was able to put my gun on Jack as he tried to bring his rifle round to bear on me.

He was close, no more than six feet away. I could see where one of my rifle bullets had hit him in the chest. He seemed to be bleeding badly. He was bleeding from the mouth and his shirt front was wet and red. He was hurt bad but he was determined to try and take me along with him.

He almost did. There was only a second in it when it came to firing the next shot. Somehow I beat him to it. I wasn't thinking much about it, just doing it. I loosed off my first shot, held the trigger back, and worked the hammer with the heel of my left hand until the remaining five shots were fired. I'm no believer in fanning a six-gun for I've seen the chaos that it can cause, but it was the quickest way to get the most lead into Jack Reever before he let loose on me with his rifle. Like I said, fanning isn't exactly noted for accuracy, but Jack was only a few feet away from me and he took every single one of those bullets. They put him down in such a way that I was in no doubt as to whether he'd ever get up again.

I pushed to my feet as the racket of my shots bounced back and forth among the rocks. My head was aching from the bang I'd given it and I could feel blood running down my face. I stood for a moment, trying to sort out my senses, and watched Jack Reever die on the hard, sun-bleached rock.

I watched him die and I wondered just how anyone could have built up the image of the romantic gunfighter, the dashing hero of the dime novels and the newspaper articles that were avidly devoured in the East, if he'd ever seen a man die like Jack Reever had. The only answer I could figure out was that if a man had never seen another die violently then he just didn't know what he was talking about. There was no romance, no heroics in the way Jack Reever died. Just a lot of blood and sounds that didn't even sound human. My six bullets, fired at close range, had done terrible damage to Jack Reever's chest and stomach. The wounds were big enough to put a clenched fist in where the bullets had come out, ragged and ugly where they'd gone in.

I punched out the empty shell-cases and thumbed fresh loads into my gun, and when I glanced up again Jack Reever was dead. I felt little for him. You can shoot a man and regret it but Jack Reever was one of the mean ones, the kind who would bite off your hand while you tried to help him. He had died the way he had lived. He had lived without pity and he died without anyone pitying him. It was hard, I knew, but it was just and it was possibly the only time when justice ever touched Jack Reever.

I took up my rifle and replaced the spent loads. As I worked my mind was racing ahead, trying to work out what was going on in the rocks and boulders beyond me. Will Pike and Ollie Reever would be wondering what had happened back here. It came to me that Jack had pushed things too far. Pike would be wanting to face me himself. I figured that Jack had been sent to simply keep watch on me and nothing else. His job would have been to observe and then report back to Pike. But Jack had taken it on himself to try and finish it. He very nearly had done. And Pike would be doing some wondering now, I realised. He and Ollie would be on the alert more than ever now. I'd cut the odds down to two but there would be no easy way out of this. If anything Judith was in more danger than before. I had to get to her and get her away from Pike and Ollie Reever, fast.

Moving off I eased my way through the jumbled, bleached rocks, my rifle held ready. Somewhere ahead of me Pike and Ollie were waiting. They were waiting and ready to kill without hesitation, this I knew; but I was in the same frame of mind myself, so it came down to one simple fact — the one who was fastest with a gun when the time came would be the one who walked away when this was all over.

I moved as fast as I dared. Speed was what counted from here on in. I had no knowledge as to the eventual plans of Pike and Ollie Reever. All I did know was that they had Judith and that they were likely to do anything to her if the thought came to them.

Trailing them was easier than I'd expected. There were few ways a horse could go in this mass of jagged rock and I found this out in the first few minutes. I realised that I'd done the best thing leaving mine behind.

Though there was mostly rock, there was also a lot of dust and snow that still lay in shaded places. Pike and Reever had had no time to erase any of their tracks as they went along. They had tried to keep to the hard rock as much as possible but they couldn't manage it all the time, and I kept coming across their tracks.

After about half an hour I paused in the shade of a high boulder. I was hot and sweaty. I could have done with a full canteen of water right then. My head was still hurting from the bang I'd given it. I sleeved my damp face and studied the way ahead.

For a while I'd noticed that the lay of the land showed a steady rise. It had been gradual at first but now the rise was noticeable, and I could see that some half-mile ahead the rim of this rock-bed was sharply and starkly outlined against the blue of the sky. Most probably the land fell away beyond that rim, perhaps giving way to easier terrain. If Pike and Reever got to that rim and onto smoother ground I might find myself left behind. Once they could get into their saddles again I would soon find myself on my own.

I pushed myself away from the boulder and set off again. I kept my pace up, knowing that while I was in the open so much I was offering myself up as an easy target. But I had no time for too much caution. If I inched my way through the shadows, Pike and Reever could be up and away — and Judith with them.

I came around a great outcropping of grey stone and almost took my last step on earth. Inches away from the tips of my boots the land just fell away in an almost sheer drop. It went down for two, maybe three hundred feet, a long slope of loose shale and some larger chunks of rock. After the drop it levelled out a little then fell away again. It looked a long way down and a rough landing. I turned back the way I had come, searching for a way through, and after a minute I found it. On my left was a fairly wide gap in the pile of close-tumbled rock.

As I was easing my way along I saw tracks in the dust at my feet. I was in a long, narrow tunnel formed by leaning rocks. I travelled some three hundred yards before I came out into the open again. As I stepped into the bright light I heard a horse snort. I sought the place where the sound had come from.

And then I saw them.

Maybe twenty yards lay between us. Ollie Reever was bent over one of the horses. The animal lay on its side, one leg bent at an odd angle. I guessed that the animal had stepped in a hole, breaking its leg.

To one side stood Will Pike, holding the reins of the other horses. And Judith was by his side.

A gun cracked suddenly. The downed horse convulsed once then went still. Ollie Reever straightened up, a smoking gun in his fist. Another second and he would be looking straight at me. The time for cat and mouse was over, I realised.

'Judith, get down,' I yelled. I shouted hard and loud, hoping that she would respond, would react fast, for there was no time left for hesitation now.

Her head came round at the sound of my voice. That was all. Then she was down on the ground.

Ollie Reever saw me too. He jerked

upright, his mouth wide open. And that was the way he died. I put two bullets into him where he stood and he went over backwards. He twisted over onto his stomach and didn't move again.

The moment I'd fired I moved off to my left, levering my rifle as I went. Will Pike had me spotted and his gun came out. He fired, fired again. I was moving too fast though and both bullets missed me. But I knew I couldn't go on dodging them for long.

Pike made no attempt to go near Judith. I figured that he wanted this to be a straight shootout between the two of us. He had a reputation to back him. He must have imagined it gave him an edge. I didn't let it worry me. I'd killed a few men myself and I figured it was a man's past that mattered. Pike had killed for money, or to steal another man's property, or because he simply didn't like a man. My killing had come about through the actions of men like Pike, men who had wanted to take what was mine, or who wanted me dead because I'd got in their way. I'd killed to survive, nothing more. Pike killed because it was his way of life, his occupation. The trouble with that kind of attitude is that a man can get so convinced he's top-dog, so good, he becomes cocky, casual, though not necessarily careless. Pike would figure me to be good, but not in his class. He figured he could take me.

'Tyler,' he said, 'I've lost some good friends of late.'

I watched him closely. We were not too far apart. Pike was holding his gun at his side, the muzzle down. He appeared calm and relaxed.

'You hear me?'

'You want me to say I'm sorry?'

'I just want you to know I'm paying you for all of them,' he said. 'But I want to make it fair for you. I'll give you an even chance. I'll put my gun away. You can draw when you're ready.' I didn't answer. 'A fair deal?'

There was a faint smile on his lips. He lifted his gun and slid it into his holster. His fingers began to slide away from the butt.

That was when I swung up my rifle and put a bullet into him. It knocked him staggering back. Surprise was etched across his face. His hat flew off. Before it touched the ground I'd put three more bullets into him. The impact spun him round and his gunhand jerked his gun free of the holster. It flew from his fingers and bounced on the hard rock.

Pike tried to regain his balance but his strength was going fast. He crashed down on his face, his slim body arching violently. He shoved to his feet again, turning to face me. He was bloody from the waist up, his face streaked and red. For a moment he stood motionless, then he fell off to one side, landing heavily.

I went over to where his gun lay, picked it up. I tossed it far away. Pike lay watching me. His mouth was slack, wet with blood, but his eyes were hard, still hating.

'You bastard,' he said. 'I had you figured wrong. I took you for a square-dealer. I was wrong. You gut-shot me like a man shooting a rat.'

'That's what I was doing. You did the one thing that marked you dead the moment you thought of it.'

He lifted his head. 'What?'

'You took that girl with you. Put her life in danger. When you did that you lost any chance for fair play.'

He stared at me hard. 'By God, I figure you'd've backshot me if you'd had to.'

'I would have,' I said, and turned away, making my way over to where Judith was now standing.

She looked tired and maybe a little scared. She'd had right to be. Her hair was loose, a faint breeze stroking it across her face. Her face was streaked and pale. The dress she wore was soiled, a little torn. But she was alive and unhurt.

I had to tell her that her father was dead but that could wait for awhile.

She'd gone through a lot. For the moment the only thing that mattered was that she was all right.

I went to her, put my arms around her, felt the trembling pressure of her body against mine.

'Oh, Brig,' she whispered softly.

'I've come to take you home,' I said.

I went to get the horses a few minutes later. As I led them back to where Judith waited I passed the place where Will Pike lay. He was on his back, his face turned towards the bright sun, his eyes wide, staring, unseeing.

I put Judith up on one of the horses, took the reins and turned away from that high, silent place of violence and death.

'Let's go home, Judith,' I said, and we moved off, neither of us looking back.

20

The winter in that Colorado high country was long and hard. When the snows came again it was for the duration. There was little anyone could do in that sort of weather. Hope and Tarrant became practically snowbound. Little got in or out. Travel became difficult. But the winter had to end soon and one day it suddenly became obvious that spring was on the way.

As the snows thawed the land began to show its greenery. The cold days gave way to gentle spring warmth. It was the beginning of a new cycle and it meant that there were chances for fresh starts.

In early spring I took another herd into Hope. Meat had again been scarce and the herd was greeted wildly. While I was in town I went to see Seth. He had spent the winter in Hope as its first lawman and by the news that had got out to us he had been making himself a strong reputation.

He had a lot to tell me and I had much to tell him. Judith and I had been married just before Christmas. She had taken the death of her father well, and after a time of mourning, during which she had lived with friends in Tarrant, we had been married. We moved to the ranch. Judith had insisted on this. It would have been what William Thorpe would have wanted, she said. We had had a busy time, a happy time. I was as content as any man could be. I had a good home, a wife, a crew of men no man could better, and I had a future as secure as any future could be.

And now I had more to be glad about, for just before the drive to Hope, Judith had told me that she was pregnant.

Much had happened since that day when I had first ridden into Hope. It seemed that there was more ahead. There would be good and bad, for this wild land and the people in it were by no means tamed yet. But we were strong enough to face it, I knew that. What we had gone through had given us the strength to face anything that came our way. Our roots were already well set, we had spilt sweat and blood over this land and we would not give up the fight to survive.

Some things had changed. Jacob had gone. Restless and yearning for new pastures, he had saddled up and had said his good-byes. It had been hard losing him but he was bound to go. We had got a couple of letters from him, the last one from a little border town in New Mexico. Jacob had a lot of the roving spirit in him. Maybe one day he would settle down. I knew that someday he would come and see us. He would ride in and it would be like he'd never been away. But for now we had to be content with the occasional letter. Sachs had left us too. The peaceful life, he said, was aging him fast. He had bought himself a mule and some supplies and had taken off into the hills.

I knew that when he tired of his own company he would make his way back. He knew that he would always be welcome.

Other things had changed far more permanently. A white stone marker just beyond the house showed where Judith's father lay. He would not come back. Nor would Joel Welcome in his shaded grave close by where the mine had been. The mine was finished with now, deserted, but just beyond Joel's resting place was a regular trail that led in from Tarrant down into Hope. A daily stage had started running and the trail was well established. It even had a name — The Welcome Trail.

Hope itself was becoming almost respectable. More and more families were moving in and the rough element had almost ceased to exist. There were still saloons and gambling halls. But now there was a church as well. There was a school and talk of sending for a full-time teacher.

I had my visit with Seth and got the

promise of a visit from him. He hadn't been to the ranch for some time but I knew that my news about Judith would get him there.

I climbed into the saddle and rode along the street. Joe Crown and Lew Riley had helped me push the herd into Hope and now they were staying over for the day. Swede and Bill Ward were back at the ranch, so Judith was being well looked after, but I wanted to be back there with her.

I put my horse up the trail and settled easily in the saddle. The sun was warm on me as I rode, the air fresh and spring-cool. My horse arched his neck and I could feel his need to run so I gave him his head and he gave a shrill of pleasure as he stepped off into a steady lope.

Like me he wanted to be home.

We do hope that you have enjoyed reading this large print book.

Did you know that all of our titles are available for purchase?

We publish a wide range of high quality large print books including:
Romances, Mysteries, Classics
General Fiction
Non Fiction and Westerns

Special interest titles available in large print are:
The Little Oxford Dictionary
Music Book, Song Book
Hymn Book, Service Book

Also available from us courtesy of Oxford University Press:
Young Readers' Dictionary
(large print edition)
Young Readers' Thesaurus
(large print edition)

For further information or a free brochure, please contact us at:
Ulverscroft Large Print Books Ltd.,
The Green, Bradgate Road, Anstey,
Leicester, LE7 7FU, England.
Tel: (00 44) **0116 236 4325**
Fax: (00 44) **0116 234 0205**

THE JAYHAWKERS

Elliot Conway

Luther Kane, one-time captain with Colonel Mosby's raiders, is forced to leave Texas; bounty hunters are tracking down and arresting men who served with the colonel during the Civil War. He joins up with three Missouri brush boys, outlawed by the Union government, and themselves hunted for atrocities committed whilst riding with 'Bloody' Bill Anderson. Now, in a series of bloody shoot-outs, they must take the fight to the red-legs to finally end the war against them . . .

VENGEANCE AT BITTERSWEET

Dale Graham

Always a loner, Largo reckoned it was the reason for his survival as a bounty hunter. But things change when he has to join forces with Colonel Sebastian Kyte in the hunt for a band of desperate killers. Kyte is not interested in financial rewards. So what is the old Confederate soldier's game? And how does a Kiowa medicine man's daughter figure in the final showdown at Bittersweet? Vengeance is sweet, but it comes with a heavy price tag.

DEVIL'S RANGE

Skeeter Dodds

Caleb Ross had agreed to join his old friend Tom Watson as a ranching partner in Ghost Creek, and arrives full of optimism. But he rides into big trouble. Tom has been gunned down by Jack Sweeney of the Rawl range, mentor in mayhem to Scott Rawl . . . Enraged, Caleb heads for the ranch seeking vengeance for Tom's murder. But, up against a crooked law force and formidable opposition, he'll have to be quick and clever if he's to survive . . .

THE COYOTE KIDS

David Bingley

When Billy Bartram met Della Rhodes, he was led to contact her brother, Sandy East, one of the Coyote Kids. Billy's determined vendetta against Long John Carrick — a veteran renegade and gang leader — made him an ally of the Coyote Kids. Carrick's boys were hounding them to grab some valued treasure, but only the Kids knew of its location. When Red Murdo, the other Kid became a casualty, Sandy and Billy had to fight for their very existence ... as well as for the treasure.

CALHOUN'S BOUNTY

I. J. Parnham

With his dying breath, a bullet-ridden man staggers into Stonewall's saloon clutching a gold bar, and names bounty hunter Denver Calhoun as his killer. Despite the dead man being one of the bank-raiding Flynn gang, the hunt is on for Denver. In Bluff Creek, when the unlikely Horace Turner wagers a gold bar in a poker game, Denver reckons that the Flynns are involved. Can he succeed in bringing them to justice though, now the bounty hunter has become the hunted?